MORIBITO

GUARDIAN OF THE SPIRIT

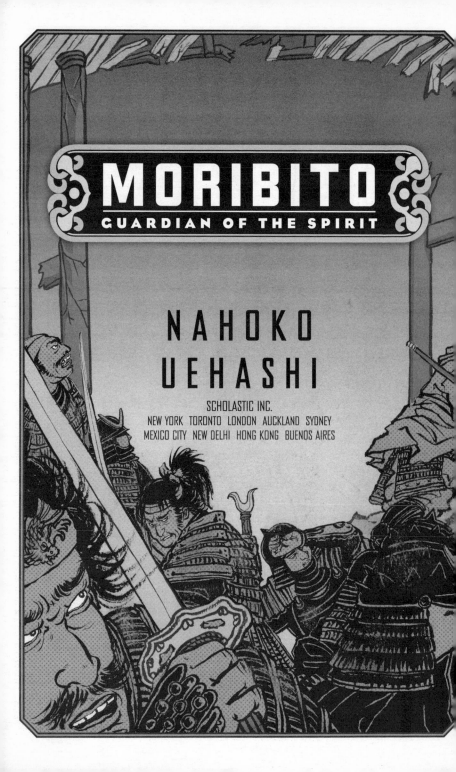

MORIBITO
GUARDIAN OF THE SPIRIT

NAHOKO UEHASHI

SCHOLASTIC INC.
NEW YORK TORONTO LONDON AUCKLAND SYDNEY
MEXICO CITY NEW DELHI HONG KONG BUENOS AIRES

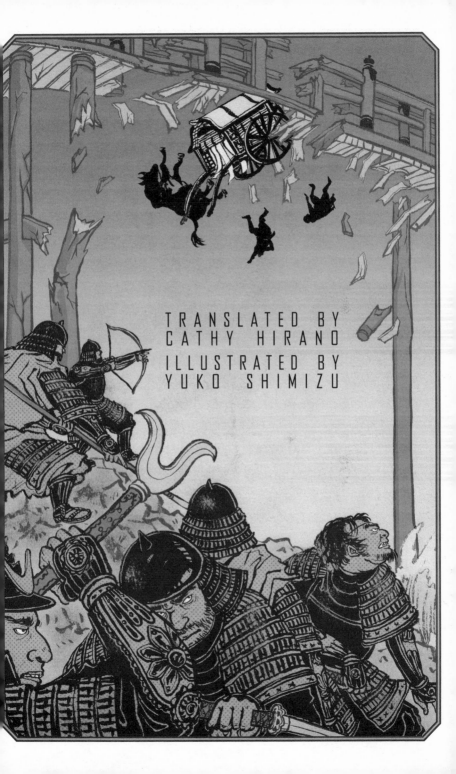

TRANSLATED BY
CATHY HIRANO
ILLUSTRATED BY
YUKO SHIMIZU

Text copyright © 1996 by Nahoko Uehashi
Translation copyright © 2008 by Cathy Hirano
Illustrations copyright © 2008 by Yuko Shimizu

ISBN-13: 978-0-545-00543-2
ISBN-10: 0-545-00543-4

Arthur A. Levine Books hardcover edition designed by Phil Falco, published by Arthur A. Levine Books, an imprint of Scholastic Inc., June 2008.

12 11 10 9 8 7 6 5 4 3 2 1   9 10 11 12 13 14/0

Printed in the U.S.A.   40
This edition first printing, April 2009

CONTENTS

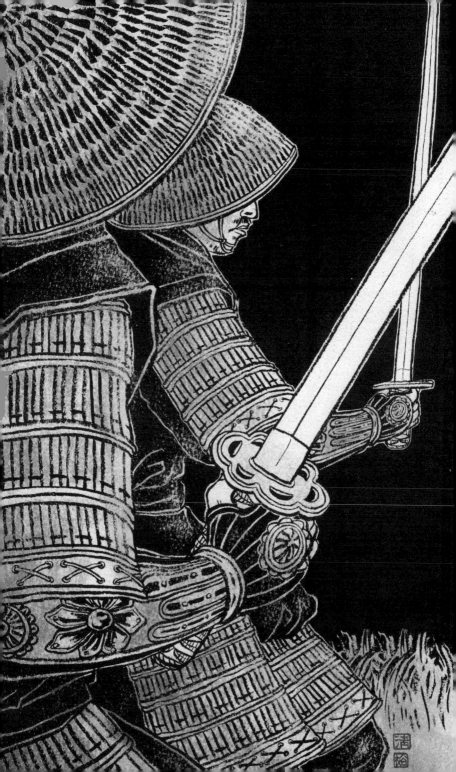

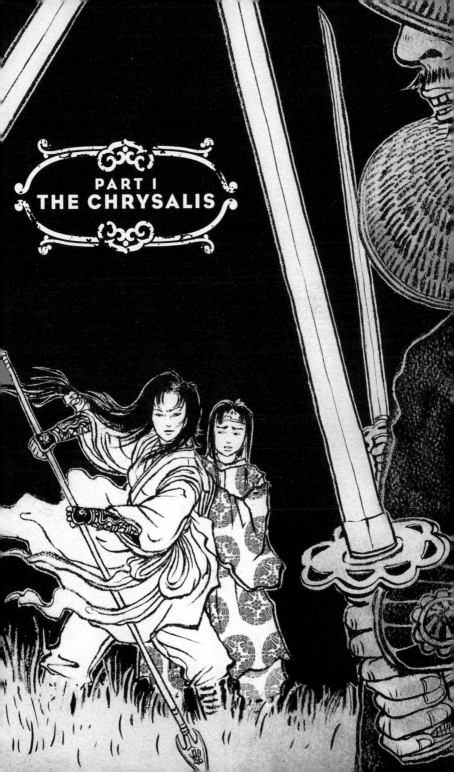

CHAPTER I
BALSA TO THE RESCUE

At the moment the royal procession reached the Yamakage Bridge, Balsa's destiny took an unexpected turn.

She was crossing the commoners' bridge downstream, the Aoyumi River visible through gaps between the planks. Never a pleasant sight, today it was particularly terrifying — swollen after the long autumn rains, its muddy brown waters topped with churning white foam. The rickety bridge swayed precariously in the wind.

Balsa, however, stepped forward without hesitation. Her long, weather-beaten hair was tied at the nape of her neck, and her face, unadorned by makeup, was tanned and beginning to show fine wrinkles. She carried a short spear over her shoulder with a cloth sack dangling from the end; her compact body was lithe and firmly muscled under her threadbare traveling cloak. Anyone versed in the martial arts would recognize her immediately as a formidable opponent. But it was her eyes that truly arrested an observer: darkest black, startlingly intense, they made it clear that she could not be easily manipulated.

These eyes now glanced upstream as she strode briskly across the bridge. Maple leaves had dyed the towering mountain slopes crimson. In the distance she could see an ox-drawn carriage, its gold fastenings gleaming in the sunset as it moved across the Yamakage Bridge — which, Balsa knew, was reserved solely for the royal family. Twenty attendants accompanied the carriage, and the red flag preceding it indicated the rank of its occupant.

The Second Prince. He must be returning to the capital from the royal villa in the mountains, Balsa thought. She paused to watch, captivated by the beauty of that moment, suspended in time like a hanging scroll; she knew that at this distance, failure to prostrate herself could not be considered a crime. Balsa was not native to this country, and for a personal and unforgettable reason, she had very little respect for rulers of any kind.

In the next instant, however, the tranquil scene was shattered as the ox hurled off the servant who grasped its halter. Rearing and charging wildly, it rushed forward and back, kicking its hooves and tossing its horns. The attendants were powerless to stop it; the animal seemed to have gone berserk. Balsa watched as the carriage toppled slowly to its side.

And then a small figure in red was flung out of the

carriage, arms and legs flailing as he plummeted toward the river below.

By the time the water swallowed him, Balsa had already dropped her belongings, shrugged off her cloak, clipped the metal clasp of a rope to the end of her spear, and sent the shaft speeding toward the riverbank. It flew straight and true, sinking deep into the ground between two rocks. From the corner of her eye, she glimpsed three or four servants leaping after the prince as she grasped the rope firmly in her fist and dived into the murky water below.

The shock as she hit the surface was like being slammed into a stone floor — she almost lost consciousness. Buffeted by the rushing torrent, she hauled on the rope and climbed onto the nearest rock. She pushed wet strands of hair from her face and stared intently at the water until she caught sight of something small and red bobbing down the river. A hand fluttered on the surface, sank, then fluttered again.

Let him have fainted. Please let him have fainted, she prayed. Getting her bearings, she leapt back into the swirling river and swam hard against the flow toward the spot where her path would cross that of the prince. The freezing water cut like a knife as it gurgled in her ears. She could just barely see the red of the prince's robe in the dark current, and she felt the cloth slip through the fingers of her outstretched hand.

Balsa swore in frustration, but in that instant, something strange happened. For a second — no more than the time it took to blink — she felt herself buoyed up. The raging river was suddenly stilled, all sound faded away; everything came to a halt within a clear blue space that seemed to stretch on forever. The prince alone stood out sharp and distinct. Without understanding what was happening, Balsa reached out to grasp his robe.

As soon as her hand closed on the material, the force of the water hit her so strongly she thought it would wrench her arm off — as if that strange moment in time had been no more than a dream. With all her might, she pulled the prince to her and hooked his belt onto the metal clip attached to the other end of the rope. Gripping the rope in one numb hand, she swam back to the bank and, on the verge of collapse, hauled the prince ashore.

He looked only eleven or twelve years old, his childish face as white as a sheet. Fortunately, he had fainted from the shock of the fall, just as Balsa had hoped, and his stomach was not bloated with water. She worked to revive him until he coughed and began breathing again.

Well, thank goodness for that, she sighed inwardly.

Little did she know that this was only the beginning.

CHAPTER II
THE FLIGHT BEGINS

Draining the last drop of wine from her cup, Balsa breathed a contented sigh. What a surprise it had been to be invited to Ninomiya Palace! True, she had saved the prince's life, but as a foreigner, she was of even lower rank than a commoner: The most she had expected was a sum of money. Indeed, when she left the prince with his courtiers on the riverbank earlier that day, an attendant had asked where she was lodging so he could bring her a reward. But the messenger who appeared at the inn said that the prince's mother, the Second Queen, wished to entertain her at the palace first.

The Mikado, the divine ruler of New Yogo, had three wives. The one who bore him his first son was known as the First Queen; the one who bore him his second son, the Second Queen. Balsa had heard that there were no further heirs to the throne beyond the Second Prince, as the Third Queen had borne no sons. Such tales, however, concerned people of a different sphere than hers, and she knew no more.

Balsa was not so ignorant of the world that the royal invitation made her vain: She knew that royalty only treat commoners kindly when they want something in return. While she was fully aware that the summons meant trouble, she could hardly refuse it without appearing rude — and that would only mean even worse trouble. She had had no choice but to come.

Still, she was being given what seemed a wholehearted welcome; the Second Queen must love her son very much. The room in which Balsa ate was located in the outermost reaches of the palace, but a large charcoal brazier kept the space comfortably warm, and the meal was like nothing she had ever tasted before: crisply fried, juicy chicken; a subtly flavored cream soup; and fine wine, served in an elegant glass goblet. She savored every dish without fear of poisoning, for she knew that if anyone had wanted to silence her, they would have assassinated her at the inn, not at the palace.

Although the queen had summoned her, she did not come to Balsa in person, but instead sent the prince's chamberlain to convey her gratitude. Balsa was not surprised by this; according to Yogoese belief, members of the royal family were direct descendants of the great god Ten no Kami, and the divine power within them could unintentionally harm those in its path, like water flowing downhill. A commoner could be blinded just looking into their eyes.

Balsa turned to the chamberlain now and bowed. "Thank you for the delicious meal," she said. "A commoner such as I does not deserve such an excellent dinner."

The chamberlain, his white beard elegantly trimmed, bowed his head. "It is hardly sufficient repayment for saving the prince's life. Her Highness asks that you stay in the palace tonight."

Balsa frowned slightly. "I couldn't possibly take advantage of such kindness. Please tell her this delicious meal is more than enough."

"No, really," the chamberlain protested. He patted Balsa on the shoulder, as if to reassure her there was no need to stand on ceremony, but then whispered quickly and almost soundlessly in her ear, "The queen has need of you. Please stay the night." Immediately his voice returned to normal. "The palace's hot-spring bath is marvelous. I'm sure you will never forget it."

Balsa bowed her head in assent. She had no choice but to accept.

True to the chamberlain's words, the bath was excellent. After a luxurious soak in the marble bathhouse — its hot-spring waters piped in, as only the nobility could afford — Balsa stepped outside and walked toward the outdoor pool in a corner of the walled garden. The cold night air bit her skin, but when she slipped hurriedly into the steaming tub, the heat spread slowly through her. White steam rose into the night air, and the red autumn leaves swayed in the hazy light of the torches placed about the garden. Above her wheeled a dark sky full of stars.

I'll just have to take things as they come, Balsa thought.

Once out of the bath, she put on the fresh underclothes that had been laid out for her, but then donned her old traveling clothes. The serving woman attending her frowned. "I set out new clothes . . ."

Balsa smiled. "Thank you, but I think I'll be more comfortable wearing the clothes I'm used to. A commoner like me isn't used to such luxury. Besides," she continued, "I always carry a change of clothes, so it's not like I never wash them."

The serving woman smiled stiffly and led the way down a long, dark corridor to Balsa's sleeping quarters. Sliding doors covered in luxurious gold and silver brocade enclosed the room on all sides. Balsa guessed that each door opened onto a room similar to her own. Her bedding was already laid out in the middle of the room on thick straw tatami mats. She made sure that her spear and belongings were placed close at hand, then, loosening only her sash, she crawled under the covers and stretched out. The mattress felt heavenly.

It's as soft as a cloud, she thought. *The nobility must sleep like this every night, but for me it's a little taste of paradise. I wonder how long it will last. . . .* Despite her awareness of impending danger, she let the warmth of the bath and the exhaustion of the day take hold of her.

Most people fall asleep gradually, drifting back and forth between deeper and lighter sleep. Even when they wake, they do not regain full consciousness immediately. Balsa, however, could drop instantly into a deep sleep, as if tumbling to the bottom of a ravine, and when she woke, she was completely alert — a custom acquired through long years of training.

She snapped awake in the middle of the night at the sound of footsteps approaching. Two people were drawing near — not from the corridor, but from one of the other rooms. Despite the caution they took, she could tell they were amateurs who did not know how to silence their footfalls. She sat up abruptly.

A voice whispered from behind one of the doors: "Balsa." She was surprised to hear it was a woman.

"I'm awake. Come in," she responded. The door slid open and a shadowy figure entered, bearing a silver candlestick in one hand and leading a smaller figure by the other. Balsa's eyes widened when she saw the pale face illuminated by the feeble light of the candle. *Impossible!* she thought. But there was no mistake. The face belonged to the boy she had rescued from the river last evening — the Second Prince.

"You-Your Majesty?" she stammered. Their eyes met, and Balsa wondered if she would go blind. But far from being filled with lightning, the eyes that looked into hers were drooping with exhaustion. The boy seemed about to fall asleep.

"I feared for you," the woman said softly. "But looking into the eyes of royalty has not blinded you. I should have expected as much from a woman reputed to be so strong."

Balsa realized that the slender young woman before her was none other than the Second Queen, the Mikado's second wife. She scrambled hastily out of bed and onto the floor where she knelt stiffly, her head bowed low. The queen began to speak in a low voice.

"Thank you for saving the prince's life yesterday. I am always terrified to cross that river on the way to the mountain villa — but you dived into it from a bridge! Four of his attendants jumped into the river after him, but only one survived. The bodies of the others have not yet been found."

The poor men, Balsa thought. She closed her eyes. If they had not dived in after the prince, they would surely have been accused of failing to try to save him. The thought that death was their only option filled her with helpless pity.

"You must be wondering why we came to you at night and why I wished to speak with you alone. Balsa, raise your head and look at me."

She did as she was told, and the sight caught at her heart. Though the queen was still young, her face was as pale and drawn as if she were ill. But her eyes brightened as she looked at Balsa.

"It is just as rumor reported!" she exclaimed. "You look so brave and bold! The serving women told me what the men said about you. Although you are a woman, you make your living by guarding others. There are none in the trade who do not know the name of Balsa, Spear-wielder — a wanderer from Kanbal fluent in many tongues, a spear-woman who has saved many lives. Is this not so?"

Balsa looked away. "The rumors you have heard are far too glamorous, I'm afraid. I'm just a bodyguard. I protect people for money. That's my job."

The queen nodded. "So if you are paid, you will save someone, yes?"

"Well, no, that's not quite . . ." Balsa searched for words to explain. "I suppose in plain terms you're right, but there's no guarantee that I can always save the person I protect."

The queen's face grew stern. "That is strange. I have little association with the outside world, yet even I know that the item sold must have the same value as the item bought. If what you are selling is saving lives, then you must save the person's life if you are to receive payment."

Balsa smiled suddenly; she had courage after all, this queen. "That's correct," she replied. "And if I fail to do so, I don't get any money."

The queen frowned. "Why? Are you paid only after your work is finished?"

"I'm usually paid half the money at the beginning of the

job and the rest at the end. But that's not what I meant. What I was trying to explain is that if I fail in my work, it means I'm dead."

The queen fell silent for a moment. Then she asked, "Why do you do it then, if it means risking your life?"

"My lady, I'm sorry, but if I told you my whole story, the night would turn to day."

The queen hesitated, then glanced at her son, who had fallen sound asleep against the sliding door. Balsa had already guessed that she wished to hire her as his bodyguard. There must be trouble of some kind brewing in the palace, and the queen, fearing for her son's life, wanted Balsa to protect him. As an outsider, she would have no connections with the court; she would be merely a new pawn that no one had ever seen or heard of. And after her rescue of the prince, Balsa must seem like a miracle-worker to the queen. *She seriously believes that I can save the prince!* Balsa thought. *But against palace intrigues? It's impossible.*

But what the queen said next surpassed her wildest speculations. "I have come to you tonight resolved to part with my son forever." Balsa's head jerked up in surprise. The queen gazed at her steadily. "I am certain that the ox's rage on the bridge yesterday was no coincidence. Someone is trying to kill him. Two weeks ago, when he was bathing, a rock at the mouth of the hot spring crumbled and boiling water shot from the spout. If he had not slipped and fallen at that exact moment, he would have died a horrible death."

"Forgive me, Your Highness, but are you sure it wasn't an accident?"

Balsa expected the queen to be angry, but she only sighed.

"That's what everyone insists. But only because they do not understand why anyone would want to kill him." The candle made a sputtering sound. "About two months ago, when we were in the villa on the mountain, my son began moaning in his sleep, as if he were disturbed by a nightmare. He seemed to have the same dream every night, yet when he woke up, he remembered nothing. But a very strong feeling lingered in his mind." She fell silent as if she found it hard to go on.

"What kind of feeling?" Balsa prodded.

"He said — he said he wanted to 'go home.'"

"Go home? To where?"

"Somewhere. Somewhere he didn't know. But the feeling was so strong that it deeply disturbed him. Soon we had to keep watch over him at night or he would wander off in his sleep. When this tale reached the Mikado's ears, he came to the villa with a Star Reader."

Balsa knew that the Star Readers were scholars who lived in the Star Palace and had a thorough knowledge of Tendo, the divine forces that control this world and the next.

"His name was Gakai," the queen continued. "He listened to what the prince told him, then stayed up all night to watch over his sleep. That night, a terrible thing happened."

Her lips trembled. "A little past midnight, when everyone else had fallen asleep, I was jolted wide awake. I was conscious, but I could not move. I forced my head to turn and looked at the prince. It was amazing. He was . . . glowing, with a pale blue pulsing light. It was as if he were a chrysalis, with some other creature growing inside him.

"Then I heard a voice. The Star Reader was chanting, his voice shaking. I saw him raise a shining sword above my son. Forgetting myself, I gathered all my strength and screamed. Instantly, the light disappeared, almost as if I were waking from a dream. Sound and the chill night air returned, and I realized that during those moments I had heard and felt nothing. The prince lay sleeping as if nothing had happened, and for a moment I thought I truly had been dreaming.

"But it was clearly no dream, because the Star Reader was drenched in sweat, as if someone had thrown hot water over him. And he was glaring at me."

"Glaring at you, Your Highness?"

The queen clenched her teeth. "He said something terrible, something absolutely outrageous to me. He must have been so ashamed that I had seen his fear, he —" She was trembling, but somehow she managed to spit out the words. "He pointed at the prince, and he dared to ask me whether the blood of the Mikado really ran in his veins!"

"But why?"

The queen glared at Balsa. "Why? I would like to know myself! No matter how I pressed him, he only shook his head. Then he said, 'Sooner or later, he who sleeps there will die.'" Sobs escaped her lips. "I was furious. I asked him how he could predict the prince's death without taking measures to protect him. But he said, 'If he were truly of royal blood, that thing would not be inside him. So do not accuse me of foretelling the death of a prince.'"

The boy woke suddenly, startled by the sound of his mother's weeping. He patted her timidly on the back, clearly trying to comfort her. Then he turned to glare at Balsa. His eyes were so strikingly like the queen's that it wrenched her heart. "Did you insult my mother?" he demanded.

"Shh!" The queen covered his mouth with her small hand. "You have misunderstood. You chose a good time to wake, Chagum. I was asking her to save your life."

Balsa broke into a cold sweat, acutely aware that she was being drawn inexorably into deep trouble. "Your Highness, please. Wait a minute."

"No. Let me finish my story first. Please."

Chagum looked up at his mother in surprise. Balsa was sure that he had never seen her plead with a commoner before.

"Chagum, you must listen carefully too. Although are far too young, you must engrave my words on your mind, and remember that you may never have the chance to hear them again."

He nodded obediently.

"I have thought day and night about what the Star Reader

said. And I think that I finally understand. He did not reveal any details to me; in fact, I think that he himself does not know what is inside my son — only that it is so terrible it will kill him. But he did make one thing very clear: Whatever this creature is, no one from the gods could ever be chosen to harbor it. Therefore, if it is inside Chagum, he cannot possibly be the Mikado's child. That is what the Star Reader meant."

"You mean the Mikado is not my father?" Chagum stared at her wide-eyed.

She answered him clearly, her voice quiet but intense. "I swear by earth and heaven, you are the Mikado's son." Then she looked at Balsa. "That at least I know for certain. Which means that some power that even the Star Reader doesn't understand is working upon Chagum. Thus I wrote in secret to a highly reputed magic weaver in the capital, presenting it as a riddle to solve rather than something that had actually happened."

"What was the name of this magic weaver?"

"Master Torogai."

"And the message went through? You were lucky. Torogai wanders like the wind and is almost impossible to find."

Once again, the prince looked bewildered; obviously, he had never seen a commoner speak to his mother like this before, either. When Balsa smiled at him, he frowned. *Not a very friendly child,* she thought.

"Are you sure that magic weaver was any good?" he asked.

"Yes, as far as I could learn, the very best." The queen looked calmer now, and a faint smile touched her lips. "This was the essence of the reply: 'I cannot say exactly what this "creature" is, but if it is the thing believed to have been destroyed long ago, the bearer will only die if he fails to protect the creature inside him. If he can keep himself and the creature alive until the midsummer solstice, he should survive.'"

"That's all?"

The queen nodded. "This reply seemed to offer only more riddles, so I immediately sent a second message asking for a clearer answer. But by then Torogai had left the capital — to go where, no one knew. Still, I was happy that there was some hope." Her eyes grew stern again. "But my relief did not last. Very soon after that, the 'accidents' began. It was then that I realized the Star Reader's words had another, more sinister, meaning."

The prince clenched his fists.

"Rumors that the prince carries such a creature would destroy the Mikado's reputation as a descendant of the gods. To prevent this, he decided to have Chagum killed before anyone finds out, and to make his death appear to be an accident."

"My father? My own father?"

The queen put her hand over the boy's mouth again and drew him close in a tight embrace. "You must not hate him. He has no choice. Listen. Should he try to help you by summoning an exorcist, rumors would be bound to spread. Then it would no longer affect just you; it would affect the Mikado's honor, his reputation, the entire future of this country. As long as you are his son, the prince, he must kill you."

Her voice shook and died away on the last words. Silence fell. Desperately suppressing her sobs, the young queen cleared her throat and looked squarely at Balsa. "I've thought about this carefully. Yesterday when I saw them bring Chagum into the palace, his wet hair clinging to his face, I made my decision. I want him to live. Even if he is no longer royal, he will still have a chance to experience the many joys of life. He will know what it is to fall in love, to be blessed with children. . . . If I can know that somewhere he is alive and safe, I think I can bear it, even if it means I never see him again. Separation is much, much better than the grief of seeing him dead. And if he is ever to have that chance, the time is now. Balsa, you are strong. I will give you a reward that no commoner could hope to receive in a lifetime. Please save my child. Protect him for me, and make sure that he has a happy life."

Gently she pushed the prince from her arms and removed two bags from inside her robe. She loosened the strings that fastened the richly woven sacks; gold glittered brightly in one, and pearls gleamed in the other. She looked up at Balsa confidently but then froze in surprise. Balsa remained totally unmoved, even at the sight of so much treasure.

"Your Highness," she said. "I've already explained that no matter how much you might give me, it's no good to me if I'm dead. Forgive my rudeness, but I must speak plainly. You have dealt me an unfair and cowardly blow."

The queen went pale and began to tremble violently. "What do you mean?"

"I saved the prince's life, yet you reward me by taking *my* life. What would you call that but unfair and cowardly?"

"I never said anything about taking your life!"

Balsa looked her directly in the eye. "Are you sure? I am of lowly birth. If you summon me here, I have no choice but to come. If you wish to speak to me, I have no choice but to listen. And now that I've listened, I have two choices left: to die trying to do your bidding, or to refuse and die now. Both paths will certainly lead me to my death."

She knew the prince was glaring at her, but she ignored him to gaze steadily at the queen. Standing as she was on the brink of death, she couldn't care less if she was being insolent.

"I see," the queen said. "You are right. I am indeed being unfair and a coward. But I was left no choice. I do not care if it is unfair or not. I will do whatever I must to protect him." She lifted her chin. "It is true that you cannot be allowed to live now that you know this secret. Which do you choose, Balsa Spear-wielder? To die here? Or to protect the prince, take the treasure, and gamble on survival?"

Balsa smiled icily. "There are three men behind me, another two in the corridor, and three more behind you. You could trust only eight people, my queen? Nobody move! If you do, my spear will pierce the prince's heart." Her spear was already in her hand; she had snatched it up when the other two had glanced away. She could feel the men's anger from behind the doors. The queen stared at Balsa, biting her lip.

"Now, Your Highness," said Balsa, "let me have that treasure and the prince." The queen hugged the boy to her and glared. "Hurry!" Balsa urged. "Once dawn comes, it will be too late for us to get away. If you want us to escape safely, you must bring a dark cloth to cover his face and tell me a safe way out of the palace. When you think we've reached it, set fire to the prince's bedroom. You can say he started it while lost in a nightmare, and the fire spread too quickly for you to save him. You must make sure they think the prince is dead! They will begin to suspect something when they don't find a body in the ruins, but the time it takes them to make that discovery will determine our fate. Our success depends on how convincingly you act your part."

The queen looked at her speechlessly. "You . . ."

The ice had melted from Balsa's smile. "I was just a little frustrated. How could I choose to die now? I am, after all, a bodyguard, and I accept the prince as my charge. Now hurry!"

Tears slid down the queen's cheeks.

They had to keep their movements secret, for not everyone in the palace could be trusted, and it was some time before they were ready to depart. By the time Balsa carried the prince to the place where the secret route out of the palace began, the black night was already tinged with the bluish hint of dawn. The morning air nipped their cheeks and turned their breath a frosty white. They would leave the grounds through the large pipe that drained the baths. It reeked of sulfur, and Balsa paused at the entrance for one last taste of fresh air.

Suddenly they heard voices in the distance — an uproar that grew ever louder, though they could not hear any words. A faint glow appeared in a corner of the dark silhouette of the palace, and then suddenly they saw a burst of flame, like an oiled torch touched with fire.

Balsa set the boy down and pulled his small body toward her. He resisted at first, but then leaned passively against her, still numbed by the sudden upheaval in his fortunes. "Look there. The boy who was a prince is dying in those flames. When the sun rises, you will no longer be the prince. You will be only Chagum. Remember that."

The boy struggled to suppress his sobs.

"No one knows what his fate will be. If you live, there

may come a day when you will see your mother again. If you die, that will never happen. Do you understand, Chagum?"

He pressed his lips together and looked up at Balsa. Then, wiping away his tears violently, he nodded once.

He has spirit, Balsa thought. She smiled. Then, giving him a gentle shove in the back, she led him forward into the black mouth of the pipe.

CHAPTER III
THE STAR READERS

The first rays of the morning sun exposed the charred ruins of Ninomiya Palace. While others picked through the acrid-smelling debris, one man stood aloof, gazing fixedly at the smoldering beams. Wrapped in a single robe of deep blue cloth, he appeared oblivious to the noisy hubbub around him. Arched brows that seemed almost brush-drawn topped his clean-cut features, and his brown eyes shone beneath them with an intense light. His name was Shuga, and he was rumored to be the most gifted young Star Reader in the country.

"It should not have caused a fire," he muttered. "If I'm right, that creature's nature is water."

Worship me . . . A line from *The Official History of New Yogo* flitted through his mind. Recently, the legend had begun to plague his thoughts.

Worship me, for I am the keeper of the water in this land. In return, I will charm this spring so that your fields will always bear plenty.

With these words, a water demon had tried to deceive the first Mikado, Torugaru. *Could that same demon now have possessed Prince Chagum?* Shuga frowned, gripped by a cold fear. *But two centuries have passed since New Yogo was founded. How could a monster opposed to the divine ruler have survived for so long?*

The Yogoese were not native to the Nayoro Peninsula. Originally, the land had belonged to the large-jawed, dark-skinned Yakoo, who lived in villages scattered across the fertile plain. There they had hunted the wild creatures and used fire to clear small plots for farming. Long ago, Torugaru, the divine founder of New Yogo, had forsaken his war-torn kingdom to lead his people across the sea and build a new country. Now that legend from the distant past threatened to disrupt Shuga's life — if someone else didn't foul it up first. *Gakai!* He clicked his tongue in disgust. *This time it seems the Master Star Reader chose the wrong man. Now look what's happened. It's made everything so much worse.*

Turning his back abruptly on the smoking timbers, he strode away. It had been his turn to watch the stars last night and he had not slept. Exhaustion dragged at his eyelids, yet he hesitated only a moment before deciding: He would return to the Star Palace to request an audience with the Master Star Reader.

Shuga fought his way against the flow of people hurrying toward the smoking ruins. Passing out of the gate to the palace, he headed quickly toward the east quarter of the Ogi no Kami district, where the Star Palace was located. Kosenkyo, the capital of New Yogo, meant "shining fan," and true to its name, it unfolded from its center in Ogi no Kami, or "the handle of the fan," at the river's fork near the mountains. Ogi no Kami was divided into four quadrants. In the north quadrant lay the majestic Yogo Palace where the Mikado lived, its roof tiles trimmed in blue and gold. In the west stood Ichinomiya Palace, the home of the First Prince, and Ninomiya Palace, the home of the Second Prince. Sannomiya Palace, in which the Third Queen resided, was located in the south quadrant, and Hoshinomiya or "Star" Palace, where the Star Readers lived, sat in the east quadrant. A high plastered wall separated the entire district of Ogi no Kami from Ogi no Naka, "the center of the fan," where the mere nobility lived. Through the middle of the wall passed the Great South Gate, opening onto the broad main street that ran through the center of the capital.

Shuga crunched along the gravel path from Ninomiya Palace, thinking about the legend he had memorized during his apprenticeship as a Star Reader. It unfolded in his mind with the scent of musty paper . . .

Once on a large continent far to the south, many kingdoms grew and flourished. The most powerful of these was Yogo, and

it was there that the great seer, Kainan Nanai, was born. Highly gifted, he could see what happened in distant places and predict the future by reading the stars. When he reached manhood, he dedicated his life to Tendo, the Law of the Universe, by which our supreme god, Ten no Kami, governs all that happens in this world.

Now it happened one day that the king of Yogo fell mortally ill, and his four sons launched a bloody war over the succession. The third-born son, Yogo Torugaru, grew weary of this bloodshed among brothers, and he declared that he would renounce his right to the throne. At the age of twenty-five, he left the capital and began living in quiet seclusion with his wife and child. One night, Kainan Nanai appeared at his door, bearing a strange prophecy that was to transform his fate and that of Nayoro Peninsula.

"Sail across the northern sea," he told Torugaru. "There you will find a peaceful paradise on a green and verdant peninsula. In that land, the voice of Ten no Kami can be heard more clearly than anywhere else. Rugged mountains will protect you from northern invaders, and the sea will guard you against attack from the mainland. Build your capital on the fan-shaped plain at the fork of the river flowing from the misty mountains. You must establish the power of Ten no Kami in that land, for you were born as his son to do his will on earth and are protected by his divine grace and favor."

The rumor of Nanai's prophecy spread rapidly. Many flocked to Torugaru's side, intent on following the son of their god to

paradise. Torugaru resolved to leave his homeland behind, and he led a fleet of ships across the sea. Nanai read the stars from the deck, guiding them safely across the mighty deep to the green peninsula of Nayoro. Torugaru traveled upriver toward the Misty Blue Mountains until he came to a fertile plain between the two rivers, just as was prophesied.

As Torugaru was a peaceful man, he had no intention of overcoming the indigenous Yakoo by force. The Yakoo, however, frightened by the arrival of strangers from a foreign land, abandoned their villages and fled into the mountains.

Faithful to Nanai's instructions, Torugaru built a magnificent capital on the plain and began farming the land. That year, however, not a single grain of rice was harvested. Nanai's Star Reading revealed that an evil spirit envied Ten no Kami's power and cursed the river's source, causing the crops to fail.

Nanai beseeched Ten no Kami to aid Torugaru, his heavenborn son. For seven days and seven nights he remained lost in prayer, taking no food. On the night of the eighth day, the god spoke: "Give Torugaru a sacred sword, engraved with my seal. He and eight mighty warriors must travel to a spring deep within the Misty Blue Mountains. There he will find one whose soul has been devoured by this wicked spirit. It must be slain with the sword and its blood spilled into the river to wash away the evil spell. Only then will this land be purified and blessed with my bounty."

Nanai took the king's sword and engraved on it the god's symbol, the North Star. (This same sword, named Star's Heart, has passed down through the royal line to this day.) Torugaru chose from among his vassals the eight most just and courageous warriors. Then, armed only with the sacred sword, he pushed his way deep into the mountains.

Upon a mountain path, the warriors met some Yakoo, who were weeping bitterly. "Why do you grieve?" Torugaru asked.

They answered him, "A demon ate the soul of one of our children, and now the boy has disappeared into the mountains, disguised in the demon's shape. This same evil creature awakes once every hundred years. So it has been since ancient times." Throwing themselves upon the ground before Torugaru, they begged him to slay the monster and save them all.

"Fear not," he told them, "for I am protected by Ten no Kami, who sent me to perform this very task."

Farther up the river they climbed until they came to a dense wood, where the mist lay deepest. There they found a spot where the water gushed from the ground. Beside it sat a young boy. When he saw Torugaru, he pointed to the spring and said, "Worship me, for I am the keeper of the water in this land. In return, I will charm this spring so that your fields will always bear plenty."

Torugaru realized the evil creature had reassumed the boy's appearance. Undeceived by its words, he swept Star's Heart from its scabbard. The boy transformed into the slippery water demon and attacked him. For three days and three nights, Torugaru and his eight mighty warriors fought the demon. At last, they severed its head and let the blue blood that gushed *from its neck pour into the spring. A flash of lightning split the heavens and struck the spring, filling it with light, and the water burst up into the sky. Purified by the heavens, it turned to rain, which fell upon the earth and cleansed it of the demon's influence.*

Thus Torugaru brought bountiful harvests to the land and became its first Mikado, our divine ruler. He named the land New Yogo, which means "new land blessed by Ten no Kami." And that is how Torugaru proved he was truly the son of Ten no Kami and protected by his grace.

As Shuga approached the Star Palace, his mind went back to Torugaru's mentor, Nanai. *The Star Readers have guided the people since the country's founding*, he thought. Nanai had become Master Star Reader, and it was he who instructed the first Star Readers in the laws of Tendo. He sought out boys who showed unusual promise, regardless of rank, and brought them to the Star Palace for training. The one who proved most talented eventually rose to the supreme rank of Master Star Reader, versed in all the secret knowledge and rituals.

Even two centuries after Nanai's death, it's still the same, Shuga mused. *While most people believe the Mikado is in charge, it's really us Star Readers, led by our Master, who guide his decisions.*

The instant Shuga passed through the Star Gate, which was studded with mother-of-pearl to symbolize the brilliance of the stars, his troubled mind filled with calm. He had lived here for eight years now, yet every time he entered he felt the same flood of peace. And as always, he thought that anyone other than a Star Reader would experience indescribable loneliness at the sight before him.

While lush green trees surrounded all the other palaces, the Star Palace was encircled by a vast courtyard of white sand, with not a leaf nor blade of grass to be seen. Every Star Reader knew the reason for this: The slightest sigh could become an enormous obstacle when trying to catch the faint whisper of the gods in the movement of the heavens. Thus, to accomplish their task, the Star Readers had to block out every distraction — not just sounds, but their awareness of other creatures and their own thoughts and desires. This was why the first Master Star Reader, Kainan Nanai, had insisted that the palace be surrounded by sand. He had also forbidden anyone but single men to live in the precincts, because family, too, could be a distraction. Married men lived in Ogi no Naka and traveled from there.

The sand shifted softly under Shuga's feet as he walked toward the palace — a perfect hexagon of white stone roofed with black tiles. The Star Tower, where Readers on duty read the sky day and night, soared up from the center. When he had first seen it, Shuga felt he had stepped into a new world: No longer was he a fisherman's son. If he succeeded in becoming a Star Reader, he would gain noble rank, a place in this sanctified world, and eventually, the power to run the country's affairs. Now, eight years later, the tranquility of that space, paved in white sand, had penetrated his very soul. This was the only life he knew.

Morning was the slowest time of day at the palace. An elderly man moved his broom methodically near the entrance, sweeping the sand smooth. When he noticed Shuga, he stopped and silently bowed his head.

Entering the palace from the bright light of day, Shuga needed a second to adjust to the dimness within. Everything was perfectly still. Although close to a hundred people lived in the palace, the sound of movement and the hush of voices were swallowed by the silence. Shuga removed his sandals inside the dirt-floored entranceway and stepped onto the chill stone tiles of the corridor. He headed toward the Master Star Reader's room deep inside, tendrils of smoke trailing after him from the incense burners at each of the building's six corners. A white cloth hung beside the door to the Master Star Reader's room, a fact Shuga noted with relief. Purple would have meant that he was meditating and could not be disturbed for at least a day — perhaps many days.

He was about to announce his presence when the door suddenly slid open. Unfortunately, the short, middle-aged man who appeared there happened to be the last person Shuga wanted to see at that moment — his superior, Gakai. Shuga bowed and drew back politely. Gakai swept into the hall, and for an instant Shuga thought that he would pass him by, but the older man stopped and stared up at him suspiciously.

"What's your business with the Master Star Reader? If it's about Ninomiya Palace, I have already informed him in detail."

"I wished to ask a question about how to read the stars last night," Shuga answered quietly.

Gakai snorted derisively. "Really? Then why do you smell like smoke?"

Shuga's expression remained unmoved. "I went to see the palace after I finished Star Reading."

Before Gakai could open his mouth, a voice came from inside the room. "Is that you, Shuga?"

Shuga straightened abruptly. "Yes, Master Star Reader."

"Come in. You've arrived at a good time. There's something I want to discuss with you."

Gakai glared angrily at Shuga before stalking away.

The large room inside the door was tiled in stone. The far end of the room was raised above the stone floor and covered in thick mats of woven reeds. Heavy brocade curtains concealed the Master's sleeping quarters on the left, while the right side of the room opened onto the inner courtyard with the Star Tower at its center. At the moment, all the wooden shutters were raised, and the white morning sun filtered softly through the opening, which was covered by a thin curtain.

The Master Star Reader was sitting on the platform in

the sunlight, his legs folded under him, one hand stretched out toward the warmth of a charcoal brazier. His name was Hibi Tonan. Large and sturdy, with broad shoulders, he looked more like a warrior than a Star Reader. At seventy-four years of age, his eyebrows had turned pure white, but his large eyes were still so keen and piercing that Shuga automatically tensed when they gazed at him; and a majesty that only came from many years of wielding great power emanated from him. But it was the sharpness of his wits, undimmed by age, that commanded Shuga's respect.

Shuga knelt on the stone floor before the platform and bowed deeply. The Master inclined his head slightly and spoke. "Last night seems to have been busy. Are you here about the Ninomiya Palace incident?"

"Yes."

"Good. I wished to speak with you about that. Gakai, with whom you seem to have been arguing at the door, just reported — with evident joy — that the prince burned to death and therefore our problem is solved."

Shuga raised his head and looked up at him. "Your pardon, master, but I am afraid I do not agree."

The Master Star Reader nodded. "Nor do I. But tell me why."

It was time, Shuga decided, to share what had been troubling him for so long. "When you first summoned Gakai and me and told us that some creature had nested within the prince's body, it reminded me of two things. The first was the story of the evil water demon vanquished by our sacred ancestor Torugaru, which is recorded in *The Official History of New Yogo*. The second was the sign of the Great Drought, which appeared in the sky at midsummer this year. Although nothing has happened yet, the omens indicate that next year there will be a drought of terrible proportions, as we have already discussed.

"I was disturbed by the connection between these two things, so I went through the records in the storehouse, and I discovered something very strange. The Nayoro Peninsula has been devastated by drought about once every century. And according to the records, during the drought a hundred years ago, a demon appeared and either ate a child or ripped it apart — a very bloody story, though it wasn't reported in much detail. This sounds exactly like the tale in *The Official History of New Yogo,* where the Yakoo claimed that an evil demon appeared every hundred years to devour a child's soul.

"Exactly a century has passed since that time. Surely this can't be coincidence. I realize how grave a sin it is to doubt that our sacred ancestor vanquished the water demon and purified the land . . . and yet a true Star Reader should never allow the fear of being disrespectful to prevent him from sharing what he has learned."

A spark of humor gleamed in the Master Star Reader's eyes.

"If I am right," Shuga continued, "the nature of the

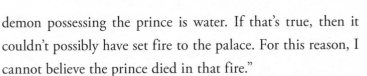

demon possessing the prince is water. If that's true, then it couldn't possibly have set fire to the palace. For this reason, I cannot believe the prince died in that fire."

For some time, the Master Star Reader stared silently at the pattern cast by the morning light filtering through the curtain. Finally he raised his head and looked at Shuga. "It seems I made the wrong choice. I should have let you handle this when you first asked for permission. But Gakai is the eldest disciple, and I thought to give him the opportunity to show his ability. My indulgence has made things much more complicated." He gazed keenly at Shuga, who bore his gaze stolidly. "You are so young, only twenty, yet it appears that you alone have the capability to become my successor. I must warn you, however: If you get involved in this any further, there can be no turning back. Are you still willing?"

Shuga nodded without hesitation. "I feel there is some deeper meaning hidden in these events," he said.

"That may be. But let me tell you one more thing. The work that must be done is not pure and noble. If you become involved, you will be forced to see the dark side of the sacred Star Palace — a side dirtier and uglier than you have ever imagined."

A chill touched Shuga's heart, and he felt his skin prickle. He was, he realized, standing at a crossroads in his life.

"I was taught that this world is a tightly woven tapestry of light and shadow," he said. "As a Star Reader, I must encounter the shadow. No matter how dark and crooked the road, if it leads to Tendo, I will follow it."

There was no longer any hint of amusement in the Master Star Reader's eyes. They burned with an intensity that Shuga had never seen before.

"Keep that thought in your mind always, for it will become the light that illumines your path. The road to becoming Master Star Reader is filled with a darkness terrible and foul. If you stumble and fall, you will be lost forever."

He stood up abruptly and raised the cloth curtain, peering into the inner courtyard. There was not a soul in sight. He lowered the curtain and sat down again. "That our sacred ancestor, the first Mikado, vanquished the evil water demon and purified the land," he began quietly, "is proof that the royal line is descended from the gods. Just think what would happen if people knew that same demon now possesses the Mikado's son! It is for this reason that the Mikado has twice attempted to murder the Second Prince."

Shuga could only stare at him in astonishment. "This is not the time to condemn the cruelty of killing an innocent boy," the Master Star Reader continued. "Both attempts were carefully planned to look like accidents. The first was intended to scald the prince with water from the hot spring, but instead he slipped and fell into the bath. The second attempt occurred yesterday, when the ox pulling his carriage received a shot from a dart as he crossed the bridge from the mountain. The ox panicked and threw the prince into the river, but while he fell from a great height, he was rescued by a bodyguard, a woman who just happened to be passing by at that moment."

"Water!" Shuga exclaimed. "Both attempts involved water!"

"That's right. It was I who planned them. I believed that if his life were in danger, the creature inside him would reveal its true nature. It seems it is indeed related to water."

"Then last night's fire! Did you order the palace burned in order to kill him?"

The Master Star Reader smiled ruefully. "It is true that I planned to use fire to kill him at some point, but not last night. I intended to wait until the other attempts on his life were no longer fresh in people's memories. Besides, I wanted to find out just what that creature is! So it certainly wasn't I who started the fire."

"Then who?"

"Personally, I suspect the Second Queen. She is a very intelligent woman. I think she sensed her son's life was in danger and made a plan to help him escape. Gakai was foolish enough to tell her what he suspected, and she immediately sent a letter to Master Torogai asking for information. I issued orders to have Torogai captured and killed, but that old magic weaver disappeared without a trace. Several Hunters are still looking, but I have had no word."

"Hunters?"

"Men who live in the darkness of this palace — assassins who act at the bidding of the Mikado or myself alone. No one except the two of us knows who they are; you are now the third to know that they even exist. You too will use them."

Cold sweat trickled down Shuga's spine. *The dark side of the Star Palace . . .* He had never imagined that the Master Star Reader would go calmly about something as horrifying as this. He felt a strange hollow fear, as if the familiar world around him had suddenly transformed into darkest night.

The Master Star Reader apparently divined his thoughts. "Do you regret the choice you've made?" he asked.

"No," Shuga replied.

"Good. There is another reason I believe it was the Second Queen who aided the prince's escape. I received a message from a Hunter who was spying on Ninomiya Palace. According to him, the queen invited the bodyguard who saved her son to dinner. She could have given the woman money and been done with it, yet she chose not only to invite her to be entertained at the palace but also to stay the night. This bodyguard disappeared during the uproar over the fire and has not been seen since."

"So you think the queen placed the prince in her keeping. Who is this bodyguard?"

"A drifter. According to the Hunters, she looks like she's from Kanbal, yet she speaks Yogoese without a trace of an accent. She is known as Balsa, Spear-wielder. As she has won considerable fame as a bodyguard, she must be a formidable woman."

Shuga frowned. A female, spear-wielding bodyguard? She must be a strange woman indeed.

"Four Hunters have already been sent after her, so it's only a matter of time before we know more. Their instructions are to find her and, if she has taken the prince, kill her and bring the prince to me." He looked hard at Shuga. "You have not slept since you read the stars last night. Get some rest, and at the third bell, come to me in formal dress. Tonight I will introduce you to the Mikado."

Shuga felt his blood race. He bowed low and backed out of the room. He knew that he had just taken the first step along a path from which he could never turn back — the path to becoming the Master Star Reader.

But right now, that position did not look as brilliant as it once had.

CHAPTER IV
TOYA, THE ERRAND RUNNER

The sewer pipe from Ninomiya Palace drained into the Torinaki River on the east side of the city. Exiting the nose-shriveling stench onto the gravel riverbed, Balsa was struck by how sweet fresh air smelled. Chagum, grimacing in disgust, tried to scrape the pungent muck of the sewer from the soles of his straw sandals. Although night still permeated the forest depths, the white mist of morning crept slowly along the riverbed, and it was light enough now that Balsa could see the pale blur of his face.

"Let's go, Chagum," she said. He frowned up at her indignantly, but she ignored him and, grabbing his thin arm firmly, began walking. He had been worshipped as a descendant of the gods from the moment he dropped into this world from his mother's womb; if she was to have any chance of saving him, the first thing she had to do was get him used to being an ordinary kid. *And that doesn't look like it's going to be easy*, she sighed to herself.

"Where are we going?" he asked sullenly.

"Hmm? Oh, well, first we need to get some rest. Then we have a lot to do. So I'm thinking we'll go stay with someone I know."

Chagum lapsed back into silence. As they walked downriver, Balsa noticed him stumbling occasionally. "You're half walking in your sleep, aren't you?" She smiled wryly. As a prince, he must have been coddled from infancy, and he was probably dead tired. "Come on. I'll give you a piggyback ride." She crouched down in front of him with her back toward him, but he did not move. "What's wrong?" she asked. "Up you get!"

"What is pig — piggyback?"

"Ah, I see." Suddenly she pitied him. Through no fault of his own, his father was trying to kill him; he had been wrenched away from his mother, deprived of all the tenderness that had always enveloped him, and thrown out into a world with no familiar faces. He must be pretty tough not to have dissolved in tears by now.

"Chagum." Balsa brought her eyes level with his and looked him squarely in the face. "'Piggyback' means being carried on someone's back. Commoners carry their children on their backs from the time they are born. If you don't understand something, just ask me. It's perfectly natural that you don't know, so don't feel ashamed. Just take it one step at a time."

She saw his jaw clench; he was struggling desperately to hold back his tears. She picked him up and swung him lightly onto her back as if he were a baby. "You'll be warmer this way. Now go ahead and sleep."

Placing her spear and bundle of belongings against his bottom, she started walking. She felt his rigid body gradually relax until his full weight sagged against her and his cheek nestled against the nape of her neck. He had fallen asleep.

Damn, Balsa thought with a groan. *I've really gotten mixed up in it this time.* As she followed the path down the river in the steadily growing light, she planned their next moves. The first thing she needed to do was get to Ogi no Shimo — the lower part of the city, where the common folk lived — before anyone saw them. She quickened her pace. A few farmers had already begun working in their fields.

Ogi no Shimo, or "edge of the fan," was a maze of winding, dusty streets. Unlike the stately Ogi no Kami or Ogi no Naka, which were built according to a well-executed plan, this noisy, coarse, and thriving community had grown up haphazardly as the population expanded, creating a tangled crisscross of roads and canals. Balsa entered along the route behind Hyakken Street, which was lined with shops. A stonewalled canal used to ferry goods ran behind the shops, so cargo could be unloaded from boats and carried inside. On a small strip of land beneath a bridge that spanned the canal stood some shabby huts, home to the poorest of the poor. Thin straw mats, hung from the bridge rafters, served as walls, and the bridge itself became a roof. Swarms of mosquitoes plagued the occupants in summer, and in winter it was piercingly cold.

Balsa checked that no one was watching her before she stepped up to one of the huts. "Toya, are you there?" she called softly, directing her voice behind the soiled straw mat that served as a door covering. After some rustling noises from within, a sleepy-looking youth of fifteen or sixteen raised the mat. His thin, hollow-cheeked face was dominated by two large eyes and topped with a mop of disheveled brown hair, and his mouth fell open in surprise when he saw her.

"Balsa! What brings you here so early in the morning?"

"Let me in, will you? I don't want to be seen."

"Sure." The boy called Toya quickly withdrew from the doorway and let them inside. The hut was astonishingly dirty. Shafts of early morning light sifted through chinks in the makeshift walls. Two thin mats served as a floor, and the stench of stale sweat was so overpowering it was hard to breathe. A head suddenly poked out of a pile of straw heaped up in one corner. It belonged to a young girl with a surprisingly pretty face, although her hair was full of straw.

"Saya," Balsa whispered, "I'm sorry to wake you up. Could you move over a bit?"

The girl smiled and nodded. Chagum stirred as Balsa

lowered him gently onto the ground. His evident confusion slowly became repulsion as he stared around the hut. "Where are we?"

Toya looked at Chagum and then at Balsa in disbelief. "Don't tell me you've kidnapped the son of a nobleman!"

Balsa scratched her head. "Well, not exactly, but I can't tell you what I *am* doing either. You'll be a lot safer if you don't know. I *can* tell you that it means big trouble and I need your help. I'll pay you well for it too."

"Oh, come on, Balsa. You know I'd do anything you asked for nothing."

Balsa had to suppress a laugh. "Thanks, Toya. You were right — this boy is from a noble family. Someone's trying to kill him, and I was hired as his bodyguard."

"Ah. I see."

The smile faded from Balsa's face as she gazed earnestly at Toya. "Now listen carefully. Don't tell *anyone* that you saw us, not even after we leave. If you do, not only the boy and I but both of you will die." Toya blinked, all trace of sleepiness vanishing instantly. "I wish I didn't have to involve you," Balsa continued, "but our lives are at stake. I'll give you two gold coins for hiding us till evening."

Toya's large eyes opened so wide they looked like they would pop out of his face. Just one gold coin would be enough to live comfortably for two years; two coins was an impossible sum. Balsa had received plenty of money from the queen, and she still had a large amount left over from her last job as a bodyguard. She could easily have given him more, but too much money would cause him more trouble than it was worth.

"You can't use the coins until midsummer next year," Balsa continued. "In the meantime, I'll give you a hundred copper coins. Do you understand? You've got to promise me this, and keep it, because if you don't, you'll be more than sorry."

She pressed a bag stuffed with coppers and two gold coins into Toya's hands. He stood staring at them in disbelief. "Am I dreaming?" he muttered. He gazed at Balsa as if on the verge of tears, and then at Saya where she sat looking equally stunned. Balsa placed four more coppers in his hands.

"I have one more request. I want you to do some shopping for me. Listen carefully and remember what I tell you." Toya gulped and nodded. "First, I want you to buy men's clothing in my size — light traveling clothes. I also want you to buy clothes for the boy, but be sure you don't buy them at the same store. I don't want anyone catching on to where we are. I also need two sheets of oiled paper, a bearskin, and enough dried meat and rice to last about ten days."

Toya listened intently to her list and then nodded once. As an errand runner, he was expert at remembering such orders, and no one would be suspicious if he did someone else's shopping. This was one reason Balsa had come to him.

"Leave it to me," he said. "I'll make sure no one catches on. Saya, give me a hand, okay?" The quiet Saya smiled and nodded happily as he gave her a copper coin. "Balsa, you must be hungry, and that kid looks like he's starving. I'll stop by Nogi's first and get you some breakfast. Don't worry — I'll tell him one of the ferrymen asked me to buy it for him." He raced outside and was back in no time with four steaming hot boxes; Nogi's stall opened early in the morning to serve itinerant workers. Chagum refused to sit on the dirty floor until Balsa spread out a small towel for him. Toya and Saya looked at each other and smiled wryly but with no anger.

"Let's eat!" The boxes were made of thin strips of plain wood. When they pulled off the lids, they discovered hot rice and barley; a fillet of white fish known in the area as *gosha*; something grilled in a sweet, salty sauce with a slightly spicy seasoning; and pickles. Chagum poked at the food suspiciously with his chopsticks and then took a mouthful of fish and rice. His eyes went round with surprise.

"Good, isn't it?" Toya said. "Nogi's is the best in the neighborhood."

Chagum glanced at him and gave a slight nod. It really was delicious. All four of them bent silently over their boxes, shoveling food into their mouths with chopsticks.

When they had finished, Toya and Saya set off cheerfully to do the shopping. Balsa plumped up the straw and crawled inside. Chagum looked dubious at first, but finally he picked up the towel Balsa had laid out for him on the floor and brought it over to where she lay. Spreading it out as a pillow, he lay down beside her. Balsa smiled at him. "There's no need to worry about bugs. It's autumn now and getting cooler. But if you don't get under the straw, you'll catch a cold." The ceiling rained dirt down on them as someone crossed the bridge above their heads. She sat up suddenly, took two cloths out of her bag, and handed one to Chagum. "Put this over your face and sleep with your head turned to one side so you can breathe."

She watched to make sure he did as he was told and then snuggled under the straw. It must have been time for everyone else to go to work: The sounds of people passing overhead increased, and their little shelter vibrated with the thumps of footsteps, the clatter of horse and ox hooves, and the rumble of cart wheels. Yet once Balsa closed her eyes, the bustling noises receded into the distance, hovering just at the edge of her awareness as exhaustion beckoned her into sleep.

When she woke, Toya and Saya had not yet returned. Judging by the light, it was a little before noon. Chagum was still fast asleep.

Pretty soon they'll realize that the prince's body isn't hidden in the ashes at the palace, she thought. *And once that happens, it won't be long before his assassins guess the truth and send someone after us. We'll have to cross the Aoyumi River tonight and make for the mountains.*

Suddenly Chagum groaned, interrupting her thoughts. He rolled onto his back and opened his mouth wide to suck in a huge, whistling breath.

Balsa's hair stood on end. A phosphorescent blue glow had spread from his chest to his throat and then to his head. Although it was very faint, she could see the light within it pulsing slowly. Chagum's lips opened and closed like a fish underwater. He stood up with his eyes still closed and began walking toward the door. Jolted to her senses, Balsa leapt to her feet and grabbed him around the waist, barely stopping him before he went out the door. As she held him, she noticed that his body exuded a strange yet familiar odor that she could not quite place.

"Cha-Chagum! Chagum!" She shook him desperately. His eyes blinked open and he looked up at Balsa questioningly. "Chagum, are — are you all right?"

He nodded, looking around him in a daze. Then suddenly he was wide awake. "Ah," he whispered.

Balsa was covered in a cold sweat, and her heart beat in her throat as if it would leap out of her body. The hubbub of the world around them returned with a rush, and she realized for the first time that she had heard no sound in the time she had held Chagum. *This can't be happening!* she thought. She wiped the sweat from her brow. Although the queen's story had seemed rather strange, it had not frightened her. But listening to someone else talk about it was totally different from watching it happen.

Balsa had faced death more than once, had even been slashed open from shoulder to belly. But never had she encountered anything like this. She discarded the plans she had made. Her intuition, not her reason, told her that they could never hope to escape by just running away. Something lived within the boy, and this suddenly seemed much more important than the fact that his life was threatened by the Mikado. If it were just a matter of fighting, she could manage; but what could she hope to accomplish against an unknown demon?

We need help, she thought. *There's no way I can handle this on my own.*

"Chagum," she said. "Tell me what you were dreaming about just now."

He narrowed his eyes and thought a moment. "I don't remember exactly, but I think it was the same dream I always have . . . Because I want to go home."

"You mean, to your mother?"

"No." He fell silent for a moment and then looked up at her. "When I'm awake, I want to go home to my mother. But in my dream, I want to go somewhere else, somewhere blue and cold."

Balsa suddenly recalled the odor she had scented when she grabbed Chagum. *That's what it was — water!* she thought. *But not just any water. Where was it? I know I've smelled it before.* The thought nagged at her, but she could not remember.

Footsteps sounded outside. Balsa swept up her spear but then lowered it again.

"We're back," Toya announced cheerfully as he raised the door covering and entered. "Sorry to take so long. We got everything. And we got some lunch too!" Saya followed him. They plopped their bags down on the floor and proudly presented each item.

"Well, that's it. Check and make sure it's all there," Toya said. He glanced up at Balsa and then gave her a strange look. "What happened? You're as white as a ghost."

"What? Oh, sorry. It's nothing. I just thought you might be our pursuers."

"Ah, that reminds me. The town's in an uproar. Everyone's saying that Ninomiya Palace burned down last night."

"Were there any soldiers poking around?"

"No, no sign of that. I had Saya go up on the dike to make sure no one was following me or keeping watch on this place, but no one was there. Right, Saya?"

Saya nodded solemnly.

"Did you? You're very clever. Thanks. You've been a big help." Toya looked very pleased. "By the way, you know Master Torogai, don't you?"

"Of course," he answered.

"Do you know where the master is? Even a rumor would help."

Toya looked at Saya, but she shook her head. "I did hear

not long ago that Torogai was somewhere in Ogi no Shimo, but since then I haven't heard a thing."

"All right," Balsa said. "It can't be helped. Forget I asked." Torogai had always been as capricious as the wind, and Balsa had no hope of finding someone so skilled at magic weaving. *I guess I have no choice*, she thought. *I'll have to rely on Tanda.* She pictured his face in her mind and sighed. She would rather not get him mixed up in this, but what else could she do?

"So," she said, "I guess it's about time we ate lunch."

Toya had brought back rice steamed with chicken. The chicken had been marinated in a spicy powdered seed called *jai* and the meat of a sweet fruit called *narai*, roasted a crisp brown, and then cut into chunks and mixed with the rice. It was delicious. There was also fruit, and hot tea in bamboo flasks, still steaming.

"Shopping is my trade," Toya bragged. "I know where to get the best quality for the best price, so you can be sure you've paid less than you would have if someone else had done it for you. And, see, I bought good food with the money left over. I know the very best and I get it for my friends."

Chagum stared intently at Toya as he chattered proudly. Noticing this, Toya asked, "Do I have something on my face?"

Chagum shook his head and asked in wonder, "Why do you speak so quickly?"

Toya looked at Saya, then at Balsa. "Do I talk fast?" he asked.

"No, not really," Balsa spluttered. "Chagum, everyone in this part of town speaks this fast. There are lots of different ways of speaking, depending on where a person lives. Merchants speak very smooth and quick, farmers mumble and speak without much feeling, and sailors who live by the sea practically yell when they talk."

Chagum listened with a surprised look on his face.

"Balsa's been everywhere," Toya told him. "There aren't many who know as much as she does. And she's very strong. She saved our lives once. Did you know?" His eyes shone as he looked at Chagum.

"Toya, that's enough," Balsa interrupted. "And don't say my name so loud."

"Sorry! In a quiet voice then," he said. "You know, Chagum, my parents left me in this part of town when I was so little I don't even remember their faces. The merchants around here are fairly rich, so I lived off the leftovers they gave me or stole things in order to survive. Saya was the same. She's like a little sister to me, so we've always lived together." Chagum listened with astonishment. "But, as you can see, Saya's got a pretty face. Two years ago last summer, some troublemakers tried to get their hands on her. It was at West Crossing, you know. Of course, I tried to stop them, but there were five of them. They beat me till I couldn't stand and then kicked me where I lay on the ground. Lots of people watched, but no one tried to help. After all, we're just poor errand runners. And they were henchmen for Gai, the boss who controls the whole West Side. . . . It was pretty terrifying. Maybe it feels good to kick someone when they're down, I don't know, but they were so wired up they just kept kicking me. But then suddenly the feet stopped, I opened my eyes, and there was Balsa. I couldn't believe it — it was five against one, right? And she just looks like an ordinary woman, while those big thugs were used to fighting. But that spear! Like lightning! And like *that*, all five of them were on the ground, and not one of them was even groaning. They were knocked out. It was incredible!

"And you know what was the nicest thing about it? Balsa helped us. Us! And she wouldn't even accept anything in repayment."

"Toya, don't exaggerate." Balsa smiled awkwardly. "I told you. I had just started work in this town and I wanted to establish my reputation. It's not like I'm some sort of hero or anything."

"Yeah, but then you gave us that expensive medicine . . . I grew up here, remember. I know what the world is like. Nobody does anything unless there's something in it for themselves. But there are some people who do more than they have to for what they get in return, and those people are kind right to the heart."

"He's right," Saya whispered. Chagum looked at her in surprise; she had been so quiet he thought that she could not speak. Saya smiled at him. "Balsa looks fierce, but she's kind. You'll be safe with her."

"Thanks a lot," Balsa groaned. "I just hope you're right."

CHAPTER V
THE HUNTERS RELEASED

Mon always felt a thrill of excitement when he became the Mikado's shadow.

He was the leader of the Hunters, an elite band of warriors who answered solely to the Mikado and Master Star Reader. Every Hunter was a descendant of one of the eight warriors who had fought with Torugaru against the water demon. The last-born son of each Hunter was trained to follow in his father's footsteps, and each was called by a number: Mon meant "one," Jin "two," Zen "three," Yun "four," all the way to Sune, "eight." Only the Mikado, the Master Star Reader, the Hunters' fathers, and the other Hunters knew these names or who they really were.

Outwardly, the Hunters served as members of the palace guard, carrying out everyday duties as the Mikado's bodyguard and shields. But when the Mikado needed a spy, an envoy, an agent, or an assassin, they became his shadows, enacting his orders with silence and speed. As all the palace guards occasionally performed confidential missions, the true nature of the Hunters' work was concealed even from their fellow guards. So it had been for the last two hundred years.

From the time Mon was a little boy, his father had taught him secretly, usually at night, drilling the necessary skills into his mind and body: how to kill a man with one blow, how to track someone, how to disguise himself. He had mastered every type of martial art, from fighting with his bare hands to using a blowgun or wielding a longsword with flashing speed. There had been times when he was so exhausted from this training that he resented his father and wondered why he was the only one subjected to such punishment; he might be forced to run all night up and down a rugged mountain path, yet he still had to wake at the same time as his brothers in the morning. If his mother scolded him for being sleepy, he could not even tell her why.

But when he came of age at fifteen, he was summoned before the Mikado, a privilege that even many nobles rarely enjoyed. "You were born to serve as a Hunter," the Mikado told him. "There is no greater honor than this. Though most people do not even know they exist, the Hunters are the true heroes of our kingdom, protecting this nation."

Mon trembled with pride at these words and entered the

Mikado's service that day. At eighteen, Mon had been ordered to assassinate the Minister of the Left, one of the Mikado's senior advisors. Creeping into the man's sleeping quarters, Mon had killed him with a single blow to the head, aiming the knuckle of his middle finger so expertly the Minister's hair would conceal the bruise; it would seem as if he died naturally, in his sleep. When Mon felt the weight of the old man's head resting in his palm, he realized what it meant to be a Hunter: Even someone as powerful as the Minister was nothing more than prey. He looked down at the man's lifeless body and laughed soundlessly.

Many years later, Mon was startled by the Mikado's order to kill the Second Prince, but he still carried out his orders faithfully, cracking a rock by the hot spring and shooting the dart that startled the ox. Unbelievably, the prince had survived both attempts. Mon had been furious at his failure — the first in his life. The Master Star Reader's response, however, had surprised him.

"You need not feel ashamed," he said when they met, the morning after the fire at Ninomiya Palace. "I planned both attempts expecting them to fail. By placing the prince's life in danger, I hoped to learn more about the creature inside him. You did well, Mon. Like your ancestors, yours will be the honor of saving this country, for I am now convinced that the prince has been possessed by the water demon they defeated two centuries ago. As I am sure your father told you, a similar demon also appeared one hundred years ago, but it tore apart the child that carried it before the Hunters could investigate.

"Fortunately, Prince Chagum has not been as easily overcome as the boy a century ago, thanks to the royal blood flowing in his veins. Perhaps this is the demon's way of taking revenge on the royal family. If so, then we must eradicate it once and for all. We must reclaim the prince before it kills him and before people begin to suspect. Go now: Kill the bodyguard who travels with him, but bring the prince back to me unharmed. Do you understand?"

"Yes."

"The water demon appears to be controlling him. You must keep that in mind when you are hunting him. And warn the other Hunters too."

Mon was acutely aware that this was to be the greatest undertaking of his life, the mission he had been born to accomplish. The seven other Hunters, all trained as he was, were under his command. Two of them had already been sent to assassinate the magic weaver Torogai. He decided to leave two more behind as contacts while he and the remaining three tracked down the prince.

On the morning that Balsa and Chagum took refuge in Toya's hut, the four Hunters set out for Ogi no Shimo, disguised as a group of merchants. They split up and gathered information, visiting people who had hired Balsa in the past on the pretext that they too wished to hire a bodyguard.

They asked about her history, her character, and people she knew in town. A little past noon, they met up at an inn selected by Mon.

"This woman Balsa has a very good reputation," reported Jin. It was clear from the information they had gleaned that Balsa was highly skilled with the short spear and extremely intelligent. Moreover, she was well known in this part of town, particularly among the merchants. While some clients were initially shocked and skeptical at the very idea of a female bodyguard, she had proven her ability and won their trust.

Mon always used the same approach when stalking someone: In his mind, he became that person, imagining how he or she would think and act. He listened with eyes closed as the Hunters described Balsa, and visualized her in his mind, letting his thoughts follow hers. *There are too many people in this town*, he thought. *But if she tried to leave for another town, she couldn't possibly cover her tracks, because there are eyes everywhere and the Mikado has surely alerted all the gatekeepers. To escape, she will have to go through the hills, over the Misty Blue Mountains. But she's not alone. She must take the prince, who's just a child, and the cold will soon be fierce. Pushing across the mountains could kill him. What will she do? She was given this job with no notice, so she can't be prepared for such a journey. . . .*

Mon opened his eyes suddenly and said quietly, "The first thing she'll have to do is buy whatever she needs as quickly as possible. But she's too well known. She can't shop for herself. So how will she do it?"

Jin answered readily. "If she can't shop for herself, the only choice she has left is to ask someone else to do it for her."

Mon nodded. "All right then. We'll gamble on her doing just that. Let's look for people who would do Balsa's shopping for her, especially someone who's buying things needed for crossing the mountains in winter. But even if we split up, it will take too long. . . . Any candidates from this morning's search?"

After thinking for a moment, Jin spoke up. Although he looked unremarkable, he was the smartest of Mon's men. "What about one of the merchants who hired her as a body-guard? She wouldn't even need to shop in that case. All she'd have to do is take what she wanted out of his warehouse."

"Hmm. Did anyone meet a merchant that she could rely on?"

"You mean someone so grateful that she could trust him to keep his mouth shut?"

Jin glanced at the other two. Zen narrowed his eyes. It was impossible to tell from his expressionless face what he was thinking. Yun scratched his chin roughly, then looked at Jin and shook his head. "I didn't meet anyone like that. I talked to Ishiro the pharmacist and Gasaku the weaver, but both were just regular merchants. As far as they were concerned, Balsa did what she was paid to do. I wouldn't trust them if I was her."

"And besides," Zen added, "to cross the mountains, she'll need more than food. She'll need furs, a cooking pot, oiled paper to keep off the rain. . . ."

Jin nodded. "Yes, I see what you mean. She won't be able to get everything at one shop — she'll have to buy things at many different places. But it wouldn't be difficult to get one of the merchant's workers or even his children to help."

At this Mon shook his head. "No, I don't think she's likely to ask a merchant, for two reasons. First, if she uses anyone from a shop, sooner or later someone is going to talk. I suppose if it were a merchant who frequently crossed the mountains, he could tell his workers that he needed to prepare for a journey, but for anyone else, people would wonder why he suddenly needed supplies."

"What if she told the servant what was going on too?" Yun asked, but this time Jin and Zen shook their heads as well.

"If there were no other way, perhaps," Mon said. "But someone as experienced as Balsa would know only too well that the more people who share a secret, the more likely it is to leak out. Besides, the Second Queen hired her to guard the prince. The queen must have realized that someone is trying to kill him, and she certainly would have told Balsa.

That means she knows she is being hunted. If I were her, I wouldn't rely on a merchant I once worked for, because that would be the first place people would look." The others nodded in agreement. "All the same, she had no time to plan. What do you think? Did you hear of anyone else she might go to?"

They thought back carefully, but no one could remember anything helpful.

Mon made up his mind. "Then we have no choice. We're racing against time. Let's spread out through town. We have to visit every shop that might sell things for a mountain crossing and find out if anyone connected to Balsa shopped there today. Go!"

Jin, Zen, and Yun nodded and swiftly set off in different directions. Mon followed suit. They had until nightfall: By then, Balsa would have everything she needed to escape. True, she was traveling with the prince, but even so, once she made it to the mountains, it would be very hard to find someone so experienced.

Time flew by and dusk fell on the town. The sound of shops closing up for the night echoed along the streets, and the light had grown so dim it was hard to see the road underfoot. Just when the Hunters had begun to give up hope of ever succeeding, Jin turned down yet another street and noticed a small shop that he had overlooked before. The owner was carefully packing away dried goods laid out on a low bench under the eaves. Among his wares were dried meat and rice, both of which would keep well on a long journey. There were countless stores selling dried food in town, and Jin entertained not even a flicker of hope, but still he approached the owner.

"Are you closing up already?" he asked. "Can I buy a little from you first?"

The owner, his cheeks covered in stubble, looked up at him. "Sure, what do you need?"

Jin pretended to be relieved. "I'm so glad I got here in time — I heard you have the best dried meat! Do you have any beef? Shoulder cut? I'm going over the mountains, so I want something that keeps well."

The owner snorted. "All dried meat keeps well. But if it's shoulder beef you want, sorry, I'm sold out. It usually doesn't sell so fast, but today seems to be an exception."

A faint hope began to glimmer in Jin's chest. "Some days are like that, aren't they? Did you have that many customers buying dried beef today?"

"Well, no, not so many — just one, actually. But he took everything I had! He's an errand boy, so he was probably buying for some migrant workers from Kanbal — they're about to head home for the winter."

"An errand boy?" Jin repeated. Someone this morning had mentioned an errand boy. But who was it, and what had he said?

"That's really too grand a name for him," the merchant continued. "He's just one of the beggars who live under the bridge along the canal. A smart kid, though, and his younger sister's a real beauty. It's a shame she's a beggar too."

A light flashed on in Jin's brain: a man's face, spittle flying as he talked, babbling as he tried to show off his knowledge. "Balsa's business really picked up when she rescued some beggar kids," he had said. "It was amazing! Before you could blink, she *flattened* these five thugs after a pretty little beggar girl! The kids ran errands in the town, they spread the word, and Balsa's reputation grew."

That's it! Jin thought. "If you have no dried beef," he said to the owner, "it can't be helped. I'll come back another time." And then he hurried off, tingling with excitement, their prey in sight at last.

CHAPTER VI
THE HUNTERS AND THE HUNTED

Balsa slipped a wooden sheath over the tip of her spear, which she had just finished sharpening. It fit perfectly, as if glued to the point. The sheath never fell off by itself, yet it would drop away with a single flick of her wrist to reveal the blade's wicked edge when needed.

Chagum hoisted a knapsack filled with dried meat, oiled paper, and various medicines onto his back. Although not heavy, it was the first load he had ever had to carry for himself. Balsa nodded. "That's your share, Chagum," she said. "I'm counting on you." She swiftly finished packing and swung the rest of their gear onto her back, leaving her hands free.

"The leather scratches," Chagum complained. Under his clothing, a thick piece of tanned hide covered him from chest to waist, matching the one Balsa wore under her own clothes. She laid a hand on his shoulder.

"Listen carefully," she told him. "Think of your body as having a belt, about the width of your neck, which stretches straight down your middle, from the top of your head to your crotch. Most of your vital points lie inside that belt."

"What do you mean by 'vital points'?"

"Weak points. If someone hits one, they can knock you out or even kill you." She pointed her finger at his body, moving it slowly downward as she spoke. "The top of your head, between your eyes, your nose, your upper lip, your chin, your Adam's apple, your heart, the center of your chest, the pit of your stomach. For men, the private parts are also a weak point. There are many others — I'll teach them to you when I have a chance. Just remember, protecting those points can make a big difference — those plus your back. If you're attacked from behind, the weapon will go right through because there are no ribs guarding your heart. But your knapsack will protect you from any arrows, and that strip of hide may feel a little uncomfortable, but it's a lot better than dying, right?"

Chagum nodded reluctantly.

"Let's go, then," Balsa said. "Toya, Saya, thank you for everything. If luck is with us, we'll meet again."

"Why don't I go with you to the foot of the mountains?"

Toya offered. "I could keep watch and let you know if you're being followed." He and Saya knew this might be the last time they would see Balsa, and tears trembled at the corners of their eyes.

Still, Balsa shook her head emphatically. "Thanks, but it's enough to know you'd do that for us. If anyone was following me, they'd kill you with one blow before you even noticed. That's what they're like. I'm sorry I had to involve you in the first place. . . . From this point on, you have no obligation to us whatsoever. If they come to find us, tell them everything you know, understand? I've been in this business a long time, so even if you tell them, it won't matter. I'm sure we can get away. Okay?" Toya nodded. "All right, then. It's time to go. Say good-bye, Chagum."

Chagum looked up at them and whispered, "Good-bye."

Outside, the half moon cast just enough light to shimmer on the surface of the river. Balsa stood still for a few moments, listening with all her senses. She felt nothing, but this did not mean that they were not being watched. The men loosed by the Mikado would not be so incompetent as to let her detect them, and even if she did, they would not dare to attack her in the middle of the city. Too many people lived here for a fight to go unnoticed, and hemmed in by houses, they would lose the advantage of numbers. No, she decided, if they were going to attack, it would happen when fields alone surrounded them. She took Chagum by the hand and started walking.

From his hiding place behind a water barrel, Yun spied two shadowy figures climbing up from under the bridge. He remained motionless, watching them move off toward the east. Mon had ordered his men not to attack in the town or near water. When Yun was sure that the two were far enough away, he signaled Jin, who was waiting on the opposite bank. The hunt had begun.

The four Hunters fanned out to the right and left, forming a large semicircle with their quarry in the middle, and began following them slowly. Each one varied his pace, sometimes slow, sometimes fast, never catching up but never letting them out of sight. This made the Hunters much harder to detect than one man stalking on his own.

Balsa and Chagum finally reached the edge of town, where nothing but the recently harvested fields stretched out in front of them. The Hunters followed them silently for about a mile. Then Mon stopped at the edge of the road some distance behind them and waited for the other Hunters to catch up. Once they had gathered silently at his side, he whispered, "There is no place left to hide. It is time."

From the moment she stepped onto the path, Balsa's tension intensified. There was no longer anything concealing them from view, nowhere to hide and no one to see. If they were being followed, their pursuers could no longer remain hidden either. This would be the place to attack.

She pushed Chagum in front of her to protect him from arrows or other flying missiles and removed the sheath from the short spear in her right hand, stowing it inside her jacket. In the palm of her left hand, she held five *shuriken* at the ready — sharp metal throwing darts with blades that bit through flesh.

The moon cast a faint white glow over the fields. Only the sound of their feet padding along the beaten dirt path could be heard. Just when she had begun to make out the dark outline of the forest beyond the fields, Balsa felt the hair on the nape of her neck rise. Shoving Chagum roughly out of the way, she threw herself to the ground as a blow dart whistled over her head.

Quickly she shrugged off her pack so it would not encumber her; she knew it would take her attacker a moment to reload. Before he could send a second dart, she turned and hurled all five *shuriken* toward him in one throw. They thudded hollowly against the blowgun as he fended them off.

Three figures leapt out of the darkness and rushed toward her, tall and spidery. A streak of white light flashed from one of the shadows. Balsa's spear whined, knocking the shining blade aside with a ringing clash. Without stopping, she swung the spear full circle to repel another sword as it slashed at her from the right. Fighting them off as they attacked from three directions at once, she lunged with her spear, twirled it in a figure eight, or spun it so fast it whistled. Each time she parried a thrust, she angled her spear so that her opponent's blade slipped off harmlessly.

But while she wielded the spear with lightning speed, she could not create an opportunity to attack. She could only thrust toward one assailant, sliding her spear across the palm of her hand, and if she tried to do that, the other two would kill her. Any one of these men would have been formidable enough, but three of them was impossible.

In the end, fatigue was her undoing. She stumbled over Chagum, and in trying not to step on him, she leapt across his body, leaving herself wide open. Somehow she managed to parry Yun's sword, but Chagum now lay between her and the Hunters, cowering on the path where she had pushed him. One stroke, and he would be finished.

But in that desperate moment, the Hunters altered their positions ever so slightly to focus their attack solely on Balsa. With a shock, she realized this could only mean one thing, and she gambled everything on the chance she was right.

Instead of protecting Chagum, she launched herself straight at Zen. He twisted his neck aside, barely in time to avoid being impaled on her spear, and the point sliced his left shoulder open. Balsa charged straight into him, applying her full strength to the wound, and the pain was so excruciating that he faltered for an instant, letting her speed straight past.

She kept on running, the footsteps of the two others pounding behind her. Something thudded into her left shoulder as if she had been punched. She stumbled, but while she knew that she had been struck by a *shuriken,* she did not stop. The footsteps behind her grew louder; the trees of the forest drew nearer.

Finally she was upon it. To the Hunters, it looked as if she had run right into the forest, but instead she grasped the trunk of a tree and swung herself around it to face them. Taken off guard, Yun raised his sword a fraction too late: The point of her spear sliced across his face and headed straight for Mon beside him. Mon, however, had not earned his place as leader for nothing. He ducked beneath the spear tip, and as Balsa spun the shaft to ready another blow, his blade whistled through the air, slashing across her midriff.

Heat seared through her stomach, but thanks to the strip of hide she wore, the wound was not as deep as Mon had intended. She did not allow the blow to check her momentum. Sliding the spear shaft through her hands, she gripped it just above the hilt and swung it out sideways. Mon sensed it coming and instinctively twisted his head away, but the hilt landed just beneath his temple, with a stunning blow that knocked him senseless. Balsa did not even pause to see him fall, but turned on her heel and ran into the forest. Yun started after her, ignoring the throbbing pain from the gash in his face, but Jin caught up with him and pulled him back.

"I'll go. You help Mon and get the prince."

They had made a disastrous mistake. It had never occurred to them that Balsa would be able to withstand the assault of three Hunters. No matter how great her reputation, she was, after all, only a woman; no one had imagined she could be so strong.

The forest was dark, dense leaves covering the sky. Jin stopped, stilled his breathing, and listened for noises. In the darkness, ears were more useful than eyes. The sound of Balsa's footsteps would give her away. But the forest had fallen silent. Startled by the invasion of such sudden and brutal violence, even the birds and wild creatures held their breath. All he could hear was the rustling of the leaves.

Where can she be? Where is she hiding? Jin was impressed. The woman had rightly judged that her best hope for escape was to remain still and silent. Even knowing that to be true, most people would find it impossible to resist the urge to run. Jin had seen the *shuriken* sink into her back, and Mon's sword must have done considerable damage as well. Despite this, there was no sign of movement. She was obviously used to laying her life on the line.

What should he do? Should he wait for her to move, or help the three others, who were wounded, to take the prince back? He could not make up his mind, and this uncertainty disturbed his concentration. He heard a body being dragged out of the forest behind him; Mon must still be unconscious.

Jin began to lose his nerve. *We've got the prince*, he reasoned. *We've completed the most important part of our mission. Even if Balsa escapes, what can she do? She's just a lowly commoner.* He made his decision. The others were so badly wounded they would draw attention; he would have to deliver the prince to the Master Star Reader himself. He left the forest, his ears still pricked for any noise. Yun was hoisting the inert Mon onto his back.

"I'll take the prince," Jin said. "I can go straight from here to the Torinaki River without passing through town and enter the Star Palace from the bank. You and Zen bring Mon and follow us at an easier pace. Don't go through the city, though — you'll be too obvious."

Yun nodded, gritting his teeth against the pain. Although the cut was shallow, the spear tip had sliced his face from one ear to the other, just below the eyes, and injuries close to the brain always hurt more. Zen walked toward them, carrying the prince. He must have drugged him, for the boy was unconscious, arms and legs splayed awkwardly. Jin took the boy from him and told him his plan. Zen shifted Mon off Yun's back and onto his own. "Damn that woman!" he spat.

His words expressed how they all felt. If it had been one on one, they might have succeeded in killing her. But it had been three against one, and overconfidence had made them careless, something they could not afford to be.

Once she was sure Jin had left the forest, Balsa yanked the *shuriken* from her back. She would lose more blood this way, but leaving it in would slow her movements when she needed speed. She placed a folded cloth against the wound and bound it tightly in place to stem the bleeding. She did not bother with the gash across her stomach; it throbbed with a searing pain, and blood dripped down her leg, but there was no time to take care of it. She had an important job to do.

When she saw one of the men leave the other three behind and head off toward the river with the prince, she knew that luck was on her side. She began to jog slowly toward the river, skillfully threading her way through the brush underfoot.

Jin trotted along with the unconscious prince on his back, unaware that he was being followed. The sound of flowing water grew louder until he emerged onto the bank of the river. The water's surface gleamed faintly in the dark. He turned north. If he followed the river northeast until it bent to the west, he would come to a secret passage leading to the Star Palace. He slowed down to a walk so as not to miss the marker, which was hard to find. The smell of the river was strangely overpowering — it seemed to cling to him — and the sound of the rushing water was so loud he could hardly stand it. *What's wrong with me? Is it just nerves? What an amateur!*

He clicked his tongue in disgust. But at that moment, a different sound sliced above the noise of the water, and he leapt aside. Sparks flew from the rock at his feet, and the air rang with the sound of metal hitting stone. A second *shuriken* shot through the air as Balsa burst out of the forest, rushing straight at him. He dodged the *shuriken,* dropped the prince on the bank, and whipped out his sword. A spear struck at him with dizzying speed, but he parried each thrust with ease. Rather than meet the spear straight on, which could shatter his sword, he angled the blade slightly to turn each blow aside, waiting for a chance to slip under her guard.

Balsa could usually strike five blows with each breath, but with her injury, she was not fast enough to get past his sword. Watching her face twist in pain, Jin thought smugly, *Fool! You might have stepped out and asked to be slaughtered.* As she pulled back her spear, he thrust forward under her guard, aiming for her neck. She twisted aside and parried his blow. Ordinarily, she would have followed through with a kick to his stomach, but pain shot through her midriff and she could only reel away. His sword arced through the air in a flash of white, and she barely managed to turn it aside with her spear. Fighting the pain, she moved around to his left and thrust her spear at him again. As he stepped back to avoid it, he tripped and fell over Chagum where the boy lay on the ground.

Balsa did not miss her chance. She struck, and when Jin twisted away, she slipped the shaft of her spear under his left

75

armpit and wrenched it in a circle, wrapping his arm around it as firmly as if it were glued. He cried out as she flipped his body over with a twist of her spear and slammed him face down onto the ground. His left arm broke with a sickening crack.

To Balsa's disbelief, however, he immediately pulled his legs beneath him and sprang back to his feet, without regard for the pain it must have caused him. Not fast enough to avoid the one-handed blow he aimed at her from below, Balsa saw blood spurt from her left arm. Now they both stood with one arm useless, gasping for breath, poised to strike and watching their opponent for a chance. Neither had any intention of giving up.

But then a silent darkness surrounded them, and a strange, choking smell filled the air. They froze in amazement. The prince, who had been lying unconscious on the bank, rose and walked into the river. Both he and the water were enveloped in a pulsating blue light, and the river appeared to climb his body, clinging to it.

Balsa was the first to move. She threw her spear down on the bank and ran into the river as fast as she could with her injuries. Once in the water, she recoiled in shock: It clung to her legs like thick glue, making it difficult to move forward. Jin, who had raced after her, raised his sword and brought it down toward her head. The blow would have split her skull in two, but at that moment, the water pulled her legs from under her, and she fell into the river. In the next instant, the water caught Jin's legs and dragged him into the river as well.

In a space filled with blue light, so silent it hurt her ears, Balsa saw Chagum curled up in a ball, like a baby asleep in its mother's womb. She clawed her way over to him and grabbed his arm tightly.

As if an invisible membrane had been broken, the sound of the water returned instantly. Balsa felt its coldness rush against her body, and shaking her head to clear it, she stood up, still clutching Chagum's arm. Chagum shook his head as well; he seemed to have regained consciousness. Balsa climbed out onto the bank, supporting the stumbling prince, and turned to look at Jin. He was back on his feet but had lost his sword and was feeling desperately about in the water for it.

She picked her spear up off the ground and hurled it with her good hand. It sunk into his right shoulder and flung him backward by its force, so he lay face up in the shallows. She walked back into the river, put one foot on his chest, and yanked the spear from his body. This was too much even for Jin: He managed to drag himself out onto the bank, but there he rolled his eyes and lost consciousness.

Balsa decided against dealing him a final blow in front of Chagum and chose instead to leave as quickly as possible. If she wasted any more time here, the other three might catch up, and she was in no condition to fight.

"Balsa," Chagum said, his speech slurred. "Are — you — all — right?" he asked anxiously. Her wet hair was plastered to her face, and she was covered in blood.

"Yes. How about you?"

"I am all right," he said. He was still dizzy from the drug and his head ached, but at least he could move.

"Can you walk?" she asked, and he nodded. "Then we'll cross over to the other bank. But be careful to pay attention, and don't let the river call you. If that happens again, I don't know if I'll be able to save you or not."

He was not sure what she was talking about, but he nodded anyway. Leaning on each other, they picked their way across, seeking out the shallow spots until they reached the other side. She pushed him onto the bank, but she continued walking in the water for some time, to avoid leaving a trail of blood for their pursuers to follow.

Then they entered the forest and struggled to keep going. Though Chagum did his best to support the staggering Balsa, he was not used to walking in the dark and stumbled frequently. *We'll never make it like this*, Balsa thought. She was fading in and out of consciousness; her body did not seem to belong to her anymore. She must do something before she collapsed.

"Chagum, listen," she whispered in his ear. "Can you still walk?" He nodded. He was afraid of the dark, but his strength was returning, perhaps because the drug was wearing off. "Then you must help me. . . . Follow the river through the forest until you come to a big rock that looks like a bear. Take the path behind it until you come to a little cottage. Tanda lives there. You must tell him . . . what has happened and ask him for help."

Everything was growing dark before her eyes. "Listen carefully. Never leave the forest . . . and always keep the river in sight. When you come to the path . . . behind the rock, walk along it slowly, looking up at the sky. Even if it's too dark to see your feet . . . you'll know where the path is . . . - because the trees are thinner, and you'll be able to see . . ." She crumpled to the ground, unconscious.

Chagum, close to tears, shook her gently where she lay on the forest floor. Then he rose shakily, fighting back his sobs. He did not want her to die and leave him all alone. Repeating to himself what she had told him, he stumbled off in search of the cottage.

PART 2
RARUNGA

CHAPTER I
TANDA, THE HEALER

For a long time, Balsa remained in darkness. She was vaguely aware of her body, which at times shook violently, riven by freezing cold, and at times burned with a heat that made her pant for breath; and always it ached with a dull pain. Through snatches of consciousness she felt herself being lifted, and later glimpsed the flickering flame of a candle in the dark. She remembered a searing agony that shot across her stomach and arm, making her cry out.

When she finally came to, she did not know where she was, what year it was, or even why she was wounded. Her eyes fell on a man dozing by her bedside, his arms folded across his chest and his face lit by the pale afternoon sun.

"Tanda?" she whispered hoarsely, and he opened his eyes with a start. He was a kind-looking man of about twenty-seven or twenty-eight. His dark, almost black skin contrasted with his brown, unruly hair, and his eyes were filled with a soft light, with fine lines at their corners.

"So you're awake, are you?"

"Did Jiguro beat me again?"

Tanda's eyes widened a little. The pain must have jolted Balsa back to childhood, when her foster father, Jiguro, trained her so mercilessly he often knocked her out. "You've been badly hurt. Your injuries must have confused your mind. Jiguro died a long time ago, remember? We watched him breathe his last."

Tears welled in Balsa's eyes. "Jiguro . . . died? Ah, now I remember . . ." She closed her eyes for a moment and saw him in her mind: so fearsomely strong and strict, yet kind and gentle too, for he had saved her from being murdered and raised her with affection.

She took the bowl of water Tanda held out for her and gulped it down. A boy edged himself in beside Tanda and peered into her face with a look of deep concern. "Chagum?" Balsa said tentatively. Memory came flooding back. "Oh no! How long was I out for? Tanda, there's something I have to tell you. Some men are after him and —"

Tanda gestured for her to be quiet. "It's all right. I know. Chagum's a brave kid, and smart too — though I admit I was surprised when he staggered in here all scratched up and out of breath! That was the first thing he told me, that he was being pursued. So I was very careful not to leave any traces when I went to get you. There was no sign of anyone

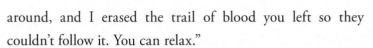

around, and I erased the trail of blood you left so they couldn't follow it. You can relax."

Balsa frowned. "How can you be so sure? You were always hopeless at martial arts. Maybe you missed the signs."

"Stupid! You know I'm better than any warrior at tracking. And before you start criticizing, you could show a little gratitude. After all, *I* gave you those seventeen stitches in your stomach, plus the eight in your left arm, not to mention tidying up that wound on your shoulder. . . . Just how many times are you going to make me sew you back together again?"

He was smiling, and Balsa laughed weakly. "I don't know," she said. Relieved, she closed her eyes and fell into a deep sleep.

The next time she woke it was already dark. The room was filled with a delicious scent and the comforting sound of food simmering over a fire. She turned her head slightly and saw a pot hanging over the hearth in the center of the wooden floor. Tanda raised the lid and nodded as he looked inside, then took some mushrooms from a sieve beside him.

Chagum leaned over to peer at what was in his hands. "Tell me what those are," he said.

"*Kankui*. They're a type of mushroom. They give the broth a rich flavor but turn bitter if cooked too long. The trick is to add them just before you take the pot from the fire."

"They smell delicious!" Chagum exclaimed.

Balsa smiled. It looked like Chagum was learning how to make Tanda's specialty, a stew made from wild mountain vegetables. He looked as excited and happy as any other boy, and she realized how tense he must have been until now. *Thank God those men didn't catch him*, she thought fervently.

"See? What did I tell you? Your Auntie Tomboy has woken up. I said she'd wake up as soon as she smelled food. She hasn't changed a bit."

Chagum looked over at her. She saw the relief in his eyes, and it warmed her heart.

"Balsa, are you all right? Do your wounds hurt?"

"Of course they hurt! But I'll be fine. They'll heal quickly."

Tanda took a wooden spoon and stirred the stew, then removed the pot from the hearth. He stood up with a grunt and came over to Balsa, deftly raising her to a sitting position, then slipped a rolled bearskin between her back and the wall so she could lean against it. Balsa looked up at him. "How long was I out?"

"Not that long. Two nights. I finished treating your wounds at dawn on the first night. I should be able to remove the stitches in about five days. Knowing you, it could be even sooner." He passed Chagum a steaming bowl of stew poured over hot rice and barley, then brought one to Balsa. "Would you like me to feed you?"

"No, I think I can manage." Her left arm hurt, as was

only to be expected, but for Balsa, it was not a bad injury. She had had more than enough injuries in her life to accurately judge how long a wound would take to heal.

The savory mushroom-flavored soup was hot and delicious. Tanda seemed to have a knack for making people feel comfortable, and Chagum was chattering away, much more vocal than she had ever seen him before.

"You know, it is strange, but the food commoners eat seems to taste far better than the food we ate in the palace. I wonder why."

"I wonder. Must be because it's hot and fresh. I've never lived in a palace, mind you, but I would guess that you have food tasters and other rituals, so by the time the meal gets to you it's probably cold."

"Of course! You are correct. I have never eaten food like this, served to me straight from the pot."

As she listened to them, Balsa made a mental note to train Chagum to speak less formally. Nothing ever fazed Tanda, but any ordinary person who heard him talk would stare at him in surprise and wonder what noble family he came from.

After dinner, while sipping tea brewed from *ramon* leaves, Balsa told Tanda everything that had happened. He listened without interrupting, nodding occasionally, but his intent expression grew grimmer as the tale continued. When she had finished, he said bluntly, "Balsa. That's Nyunga Ro Im."

"What?"

"That — thing — in the boy, it's Nyunga Ro Im, or at least, that's what the Yakoo call it. It means the Water Guardian. You said that in his sleep he starts walking toward water, right? That you saw a blue light coming from him and the water in the river changed?"

"Yes, it seems to happen when he's asleep or unconscious. Did you notice anything like that in the last two nights?"

"No. Nothing. Maybe we're too far from the river."

Chagum was listening to their conversation with a frown.

"And what is this Nyunga-whatever? Is it some kind of river spirit?" Balsa asked.

"I don't know much about it myself. But surely you've heard the legend of Torugaru, the Mikado's sacred ancestor, and how he founded this country by slaying a water demon."

"Yes, I know the story. But he killed the demon, didn't he? So how could it show up now?"

Tanda started to speak and then hesitated. "It's rather complicated."

"That's okay. Tell me what you know. It's going to be a long night anyway."

Tanda had been gazing steadily at Chagum, but he nodded as if he had made a decision. "Chagum, what I am about to say may make you angry, but you have to know sometime. Will you be patient and hear me out?"

Although he looked anxious, Chagum nodded.

"All right then. Long, long ago, only the Yakoo lived in this land. They knew that there were two worlds, the one that we can see, called Sagu, and another, invisible world, called Nayugu. I want you to understand that this is not the world that the Yogoese call the 'Other World' — it isn't heaven or hell, where the souls of the dead go. Sagu and Nayugu exist together in the same place, here, now. You see?

"The most important thing to understand is that these two worlds are interconnected, each supporting the other, although not even the Yakoo are sure how. But there is one thing they know for certain, and you must remember this well. There lives in Nayugu a creature capable of changing the weather in both worlds. The Yakoo believe that once every hundred years, this creature lays an egg. The year after that there is a bad drought. If the egg doesn't hatch by the full moon of the summer solstice, the drought will continue and bring on disaster.

"There is another important point to this story. For some reason, this creature, which the Yakoo call Nyunga Ro Im, lays its egg in a creature of Sagu."

Balsa and Chagum gaped at him. "Do you mean to say that this Nyunga Ro Im has laid an egg in Chagum?" she breathed.

Chagum pressed both hands to his chest and looked like he was going to be sick. He stood up suddenly and dashed outside. Tanda followed him, and after a few moments, they returned together, Chagum looking very pale. Tanda rubbed his back gently with one large hand.

"I'm sorry," he said to the boy. "It's not a very pleasant story for you. But I want you to know that the Yakoo regard Nyunga Ro Im as something very special. The child chosen to bear the egg was known as the Nyunga Ro Chaga, the Guardian of the Spirit — or as you would call it, the Moribito. The child was always protected very carefully."

"But Tanda, wait a minute," Balsa said. "That's very different from the legend of Mikado Torugaru conquering the water spirit. In that story, the child's parents wept because the child who bore the water spirit would die, and they *begged* Torugaru to kill the monster. Isn't that right?"

Tanda looked troubled. "That's what I meant when I said my story might make Chagum angry."

"Oh, I see." Balsa nodded.

Chagum, pale-faced, glared at her indignantly. "What do you see? I will not become angry. Tell me."

Balsa sighed. "Chagum, no matter where you go, you'll find that people in high positions like to make themselves look good. A general, for example, must always be a hero, because who will respect him if he is a coward? I've traveled to many countries and heard many stories, and a victory in battle is always the general's, even when it's won by the hard work of ordinary soldiers. And when time passes, these stories often develop into legends."

"So, you are saying that our sacred ancestor, the first Mikado, also told such lies?" Chagum asked sternly.

Balsa hesitated and glanced at Tanda. The boy was wiser than his eleven years, and therefore the pain the truth would cause him would be deeper. But she was sure that he could face this. "I don't want to lie to you," she said. "So I'm going to speak to you as if you were a grown man. The legend of your sacred ancestor probably has some truth to it. But I'm now convinced some parts of it are false."

"Why do you believe the Yakoo legend rather than the legend of our sacred ancestor?" he demanded.

Balsa looked at him in surprise, and a smile, unbidden, touched her lips. He really was a tough kid. "For two reasons. First, I know Tanda very well. He is a deep thinker, and he rarely makes mistakes. Second, from my own experience, the strong usually manipulate the legends of the weak to fit their own wishes, not the other way around."

Tanda had been listening to the two of them talk with some amusement, but here he interrupted. "No, Balsa. Although that's true sometimes, I think the oppressed often embellish their legends too. If they didn't, they couldn't keep their pride. But I don't think the story of Nyunga Ro Im is one of those. It was passed down centuries before the first Mikado ever came, so it's not likely that it was purposely changed to resist the kingdom of New Yogo. Besides, there's something I haven't told you yet."

He looked at Chagum. "I'm sure you can see by the color

of my skin that Yakoo blood runs in my veins. My grandmother on my mother's side was Yakoo. She told me a very frightening story she heard when she was a child from her grandfather, which would make him my great-great-grandfather. It went like this.

"One hundred years after your sacred ancestor killed the water spirit, the spirit laid its egg in the son of my great-great-grandfather's good friend. This friend was Yakoo, but his wife was Yogoese, so the blood of both peoples ran in the child's veins. My great-great-grandfather and all the villagers tried desperately to save the boy, but they failed and he died."

"Why? How did he die?" Balsa asked, but Tanda shook his head.

"My grandmother only told me this story after her memory had gotten hazy. I don't know the details. She said he was killed by Rarunga, the Egg Eater, but I don't know if that meant the Mikado's men, who were trying to protect the legend of the first Mikado, or if it was something else. Master Torogai thinks Rarunga was a creature of Nayugu, the unseen world."

Chagum's face had turned chalk white, but his voice was calm. "Master Torogai? The magic weaver to whom my mother sent a letter?"

"That's right," Balsa said. "Torogai is Tanda's teacher, and probably the greatest living magic weaver in the world."

Chagum stared at Tanda, his eyes round. Tanda scratched his head, embarrassed. "Master Torogai is part Yakoo too, you see," he said.

"But I heard the Yakoo were illiterate. How can someone who cannot read possibly be wise?" Chagum asked suspiciously.

Tanda smiled. "They may not know how to read, but the Yakoo know a lot about this world. Think about it. The Yakoo have lived here for ages. Any person knows his own home better than a stranger."

Balsa clenched her hands on her knees. "We've got to find Torogai, or else another Yakoo who knows more about this water spirit. I haven't a hope of protecting Chagum if I don't even know what the Rarunga is. If it really is the Mikado's men, then there are steps I can take, but if not, the task is beyond me."

Tanda nodded but frowned. "I've been thinking the same thing. But Master Torogai is so unpredictable, there's no way to get in touch. As for the Yakoo, we've had so much intermarriage that we're all mixed with Yogoese or Kanbalese blood, like me . . . We've forgotten our heritage. I don't know if there's anyone left who knows about Nyunga Ro Im."

"Well, we have to try. What about the descendants of your great-great-grandfather's friend? They might know more about the story."

"You're right. I'll check that out first thing in the morning." Chagum was still looking pale, and Tanda placed his hand on his shoulder. "I know you must be terrified, but I'm sure we'll find a way to protect you. And I'm not just saying that to make you feel better! Think about it: Nyunga Ro Im would have disappeared long ago if none of its eggs had survived. Obviously some of them must have hatched, even if we've never heard of them. Besides, if the spirit just laid its eggs in children for them to be killed, why would the Yakoo have treated it with such reverence?"

Balsa thought privately that they might have considered these children necessary sacrifices to avert disastrous drought, but she kept her mouth shut. Chagum must already be frightened to death; she didn't want to make him suffer any more. Chagum, however, said in a surprisingly steady voice, "That is what the magic weaver told my mother. The one who carries the creature only dies if he fails to protect it."

Balsa looked up in shock; she had forgotten that. A faint hope blossomed in her heart. "You're right. I remember your mother telling us that. Tanda!"

"I'm with you. We need to find Torogai."

"I'm sure Torogai escaped. That sly old magic weaver would have been the first to guess what the Mikado would do."

"And therefore be on the other side of the Misty Blue Mountains by now."

They looked at each other. Balsa whispered, "I didn't want to get you involved in this."

Tanda laughed. "Don't worry. I should be thanking you for getting me involved. This may just provide me with answers to a lot of questions."

"What do you want to know, Tanda?" Chagum asked.

Tanda searched for words. "Many things. Though I may not seem like much, I want to be a magic weaver. For that, it's important to know about the world — and not just Sagu, the world we can see, but the invisible world of Nayugu."

Balsa grinned and said, "He's always wanted to know everything ever since he was a kid. He was never any good at martial arts, but when it came to medicines or spirits, he had amazing concentration. He can't make his living yet as a magic weaver, but he does very well selling herbs. And when you do become a famous magic weaver, Tanda, you better charge those rich people lots of money and treat me to a fancy dinner."

"Don't be an idiot. You're lucky I'm still unknown and I sew up your wounds for free! When I become a famous magic weaver, I'll charge you a gold coin for every stitch."

Chagum looked from Balsa to Tanda and said, "Have you known each other since you were children?"

"Since we were this high!" they chimed in unison, placing their hands about waist height. The gesture and even the expressions on their faces were identical. They laughed.

"Balsa was the foster child of Jiguro, a wandering

warrior," Tanda told Chagum. "They came here when she was about ten and stayed for several years to train. Jiguro was a hard teacher, and sometimes Balsa was badly injured. Whenever that happened, Torogai, who used to live here, would patch her up. Jiguro paid in cash, and for a magic weaver who didn't want much to do with the villagers, this was convenient."

"Jiguro knew Torogai could sew me back together again, so he didn't worry about drilling me to death. Honestly!" Balsa grumbled. "Was that any way to treat a beautiful young girl?"

Tanda ignored her and continued. "I'm two years younger than Balsa. When I was a kid, I used to sneak away from my farm chores when my parents weren't looking and hang around Torogai's place. That's how I met Balsa. Torogai was one shrewd old woman."

"What?!" Chagum burst out. "You mean the magic weaver is a *woman*?!"

"That's right," Balsa replied. "The Yakoo call anyone with great ability 'Master,' regardless of their gender. And Torogai is one tough, clever old lady who doesn't mince words. She must have been fifty-five or fifty-six then, so I guess she's around seventy now, don't you think?"

"Yeah, I think she just turned seventy," Tanda agreed.

"Then she will never get away!" Chagum cried. "She is too old to run! She cannot possibly escape the kind of men who attacked us, can she?"

"You bet she can!" Balsa and Tanda said at once.

"If anyone can, she can," Balsa added. "She may be old, but she's more goblin than human."

Tanda laughed wryly. "Balsa, if Torogai finds out what you just said, you can give up any hope of her helping us. And besides, when you get old, you're going to be just like her."

They teased each other lightly as they shared memories of their past. The hollow loneliness that had ached inside Chagum since he parted from his mother gradually began to ease. His home was now this simple hut: a single room, floored by wooden planks and dirt, with a hearth set in the middle. Yet it was dear to him. The fire crackling in the hearth warmed the entire room, comforting him. For the first time since he had left the palace, he felt safe.

C H A P T E R   I I
TOROGAI, THE MAGIC WEAVER

In the heart of the Misty Blue Mountains, a tiny old woman in a rough hemp tunic was weaving magic. Unruly wisps of white hair framed her wrinkled brown face, with its wide nostrils, tight puckered lips, and black eyes that glittered in narrow slits; but while this face was hideously ugly, it also suggested hidden power. This was Torogai, the very woman Balsa and Tanda sought.

She was sitting on the edge of a spring wreathed in ferns, stretching her wrinkled bony legs out between the damp rocks, her eyes half-closed. Only her hands moved, caressing a rock and drumming on its surface — *ta-tap, tap, ta-tap* — her fingers playing the rock as if it were an instrument. All the while she whispered in her mind,

"Oh, Water Dwellers of Nayugu.
Oh, Shining Ones who live in water.
Oh, Long Ones. Oh, Undulating Ones.
Come and speak with me.

I am of the Land Dwellers of Sagu,
one who walks the lands of Sagu,
who lives above the earth.
The year of Nyunga Ro Im has come —
the time when Sagu and Nayugu intertwine.
Come speak to me. Come tell me."

Suddenly, she heard a noise from the spring where it flowed from between the ferns: *ta-tap, tap, ta-tap*. It was identical to the rhythm she was drumming on the rock and came back to her with a hollow sound, like an echo from inside a cave. The air around her grew dim, as if the sunlight no longer reached her, as if the color of the very air around her changed. As she listened, the sound echoing from the water began to form words in her mind.

"Oh, Child of the Land Dwellers of Sagu.
Oh, Child of the Dry Ones who live on the earth.
Oh, Child of the Free-Roaming Ones,
the Wielders of Fire.

I have come in answer to your call.
I am of the Water Dwellers of Nayugu,
one who lives in the waters of Nayugu."

The outline of Torogai's body faded as if she were evaporating. A blue light drifted over the spring's surface, blurring the boundary between water and air. She knelt down and pressed her face into the space where the two joined. Something gradually began to emerge from the blue haze. The sandy bottom of the shallow spring vanished, and in its place blue-green water, so beautiful it made her heart ache, extended deep, deep below. From its depths appeared something that resembled a human in shape, but its hair was like seaweed, and a slimy bluish-white film covered its skin. Its eyes were lidless, its mouth lipless, and it had only two small holes for a nose.

"Well met, Yona Ro Gai, Water Dweller," Torogai said, her face pressed close to the other's.

"To Ro Gai, Land Dweller, speak with me," the creature responded.

Torogai nodded. Sweat beaded her brow; it was exhausting to keep her face between two worlds in this way. "Yona Ro Gai, listen. Has Nyunga Ro Im, the Water Guardian, laid its egg?"

"Yes. Five eggs in Nayugu and one in Sagu."

"Is Rarunga on the move?"

The creature shuddered. "Yes. Two of the eggs laid in Nayugu are already gone. Rarunga ate them. The eggs laid in Nayugu are food for Rarunga."

"How does it find them?"

"I do not know."

"Who can tell me more about Rarunga?" It was so hard to breathe that Torogai's face contorted with the strain.

"Rarunga is an earth spirit. You must ask the Juchi Ro Gai, the Mud Dwellers of Nayugu." The water creature was obviously finding it a struggle too. Her mouth opened and closed, like a fish out of water.

"Where must I go to speak with the Juchi Ro Gai?"

"To the crack in the Earth — where Sagu and Nayugu meet. . . ." And with those words, the Yona Ro Gai vanished. The blue light disappeared at the same time, and the smell of the damp air returned.

Torogai gasped for breath and sprawled backward to lean spread-eagled against a rock. "Damn! That almost killed me!" she grumbled. "And now the Yona Ro Gai tells me I have to do it again! I bet it's no easier talking to the Mud Dwellers either. What accursed magic!" Her huge nostrils flared and quivered. "And those tiresome hounds are still on my trail. Pah! How they stink. I've had enough of their foul smell. Maybe I should kill them right now." She spat out the last words but then shook her head. "No, that won't do. I need to have a little chat with those Star Readers first. Their heads are so stuck in the clouds they can't see the ground. What a pain! Nyunga Ro Im sure chose a rotten time to lay its eggs. Why couldn't it have done it when I was a bit younger?"

She grabbed a handful of mud and began kneading it in both hands, all the while muttering complaints. Scowling, she yanked a strand of hair from her head and buried it in the ball of mud, which she shaped into a clay doll. Occasionally she removed something from inside her robe and kneaded it into the figurine. When it was complete, she stopped and stared intently at the roots of a camphor tree some distance away. "You there!" she yelled suddenly. "Out you come!"

The bushes swayed and a Hunter stepped out, a *shuriken* grasped in his hand. As he sneered at her, a weighted chain flew at Torogai from behind: A second Hunter had snuck up on her. She dodged the chain and leapt into the air, as agile as a monkey. But the Hunters had foreseen this move, and before she could swing herself up onto a tree branch, *shuriken* had lodged themselves in her wrist and thigh. She fell to the ground with a shriek.

The two Hunters rushed toward her where she sprawled helplessly on her back. One grabbed her arms and held them firmly while the other drew his short sword, placed a foot on her stomach, and slit her throat.

Her head disintegrated into a pile of dirt.

The Hunters jumped back and stared in amazement as the old woman's body crumbled before their eyes. Then suddenly the man who had slit her throat threw back his head, tore at the air with his hands, and fell over backward, frothing at the mouth. His arms and legs twitched convulsively. The other Hunter somersaulted away from the spot. Jumping over a rock, he sprang up and grabbed a tree branch, but before he could swing himself to the next tree, his body became as heavy as lead. His skin grew cold; a white light flickered before his eyes. His heart beat like a drum, pounding in his ears. Breaking out into a cold sweat, he fell to the ground, his arms flailing uselessly.

The old woman slid easily down from the tree. "Beautiful flowers have thorns. Clay dolls have thorns too, stupid dogs." She grinned and kicked the man where he lay unconscious. "If you want to catch old Torogai, you'd better learn all her tricks!" From the moment she called out to them, the Hunters had fallen under her spell. Hypnotized by her voice, they saw only the doll, and convinced that it was Torogai, they attacked. But as soon as they touched it, the drug-smeared thorns hidden inside pricked their skin.

"You should be grateful," she told the Hunter as she undid his belt. "I could have smeared those thorns with a poison that meant instant death, but instead I chose something that would only knock you out. Very kind of me!" The magic weaver took off the man's jacket. In his waist pouch she found a bamboo writing case containing a brush and ink. Opening the ink vessel, she dipped the brush in it and began writing smoothly on the inside of his jacket. When she had finished, she dressed him once again.

"Make sure you deliver my message like a good little hound." She slapped his chest. Then, as if an idea had come to her, she felt once again in the little pouch attached to his belt and drew out two silver pieces. Her face broke into a smile. "You're pretty flush in the pocket, aren't you now? I'll just take this in return for you trying to slit my throat. Now I can go into town and drink some good wine for a change. I might even go to the White Deer for some hot venison stew."

Pleased with herself, she chuckled, then suddenly clapped her hands together. "Wait! I've got an even better idea! There's no need for me to tax my poor old body. I can watch my apprentice do the work while I eat good food. Yes, it'll be excellent training for him too. What a splendid idea! It seems I think better when I'm being chased by smelly old mutts."

She disappeared into the forest, still muttering to herself.

CHAPTER III
TOROGAI'S MESSAGE

Beneath the Mikado's sleeping chamber was a secret room known only to the Mikado, the Master Star Reader, and the Hunters, and at the moment, it was steeped in a silence heavy with anger and frustration. The Mikado sat partially concealed behind a thin bamboo screen, the Master Star Reader and Shuga in front, as the three men listened to Mon's report.

That he and his men had let the prince slip through their hands was an unforgivable blunder by itself, but then the Hunters who had gone after the magic weaver had fallen easily into her trap and come back empty-handed. Their failure was so dismal that Mon could see no choice but to pay for it with his life. He had woken several hours after his confrontation with Balsa and was still plagued by a splitting headache and dizziness. His face was so pale he looked as if he were already dead.

"How can this have happened?" the Master Star Reader said bitterly. "One of you is slashed across the face, another stabbed in the shoulder, and yet another so badly wounded he will be lucky to survive. And you, their leader, were hit in the head and knocked senseless." Mon could say nothing. "Was this woman really such a dangerous foe?"

Thinking back on it, Mon realized that what made her dangerous was her fearless disregard for personal injury. "She saw my sword thrust coming, yet she didn't even try to dodge the blow. Most people, no matter how brave, would instinctively try to block it. Yet she chose to hit me in the head instead of avoiding my blade — without even stopping to think. You can't do that consciously. You can't do it by steeling yourself for the hit, either. You would have to be used to it, to have been cut again and again since you were a child."

A cold voice came from behind the bamboo screen. "What you mean is that you, the Head of the Hunters, have less skill than a woman." Mon did not raise his head. Though he could not see it, the Mikado's thin elegant face was trembling with rage. Never in his life had his will been thwarted. This was the first time anyone had failed to carry out his wishes. He was seized by an urge to strike Mon where he knelt with his forehead pressed against the floor. He was smart enough, however, to suppress his feelings, though he barely managed it. "What is worse, the men you sent after that Yakoo magic weaver came back with their tails between their legs. Never in all our history has a Mikado had such incompetent Hunters."

These last words, which were almost spat out, cut Mon to the heart. At that moment, he heard a faint rapping on the door to the underground passage. Recognizing it as the Hunters' secret signal for urgent business, he bowed in apology, stood up, and went to open the door. One of the Hunters who had tried to kill Torogai stood pale-faced in the corridor. "What do you want?" Mon snapped.

The Hunter flinched and showed him his jacket turned inside out. "When I was changing, I noticed this message. It appears to be from Torogai."

Mon snatched the garment from his hands. It was true: There were letters written on it. He glared at the Hunter, hot anger burning inside him. Only the presence of the Mikado stopped him from hitting the man. "Go," he barked, and the Hunter fled.

"What is it?" the Mikado demanded.

Mon prostrated himself on the floor and said, "There's a message from Torogai on the inside of the Hunter's jacket."

The Mikado and the Master Star Reader glanced at one another through the screen. Then the Master Star Reader stood up and took the jacket from Mon, making a gesture to ward off evil spells as he did so. "It may be cursed. Let me see it first." As he read the difficult handwriting, the frown between his eyes deepened.

"What does it say?" the Mikado asked impatiently.

The Master Star Reader groaned. "It is just as well that I read this first. As I feared, it casts a curse on the Mikado. I must reverse the curse immediately and burn it." He turned the garment right side out, so that the writing was on the inside, and folded it carefully. "Your Highness, give me leave to work on this until tomorrow. To make haste is to risk failure. Shuga and I will need a little more time to think." Bowing, he took Shuga and exited the room, leaving behind the Mikado and Mon, who both longed to ask more questions.

The Master Star Reader did not say another word until he had returned to his own room in the Star Palace. Only after he was inside and had made sure that no one was nearby did he finally speak. "Curse that Yakoo magic weaver! She's left us a strange message." He handed the jacket to Shuga. "Here. Read it yourself. There was no curse on it." Shuga took it and began reading the scrawled letters.

My dear Star Readers,

Are you so busy with the stars and your little games that you've forgotten where you are? We stand at a turning point that comes once a century. Instead of wasting your time on me, protect the egg — it's hidden in one of your people, after all! If you fail, a terrible drought will strike the land.

The egg-stealing Rarunga is awake and has already begun to seek the egg. Two centuries ago, your ancestors were smart enough to join the Yakoo and destroy Rarunga. Though I hate to admit it, my dear Star Readers, we Yakoo have also left precious knowledge back beyond the ends of time. We have forgotten how to slay Rarunga. If by any chance you have preserved this knowledge, then hurry! Quit watching the sky and turn your eyes to the land. Come and kill the Egg Eater!

Torogai

Shuga read it twice and then looked up at the Master Star Reader, puzzled. "Surely she is making fun of us." The tone of the message was not just confident, but insolent and cocky. The men who read the stars were revered; even the Mikado followed their advice. Never had Shuga run into anyone who dared to refer to them so cheekily as "my dear Star Readers." She was nothing more than a Yakoo magic weaver, yet she addressed them as if speaking to her equals. "Who is this Torogai? From her letter, it sounds like she knows much more than we do about the water demon."

The Master Star Reader folded his arms. "That's because she's a magic weaver with Yakoo blood in her veins. She probably knows a lot about the demons and spirits that dwell in this land."

"She tells us to 'protect the egg,' but in the legend of our sacred ancestor, weren't the Yakoo afraid of the water demon? And she writes as if the Master Star Reader Nanai joined the Yakoo to destroy this thing she calls Rarunga, the Egg Eater." Shuga stopped suddenly, struck by a possibility that made him shiver. "It can't be," he whispered.

"What can't be?" The Master Star Reader stared at him intently, his eyes cold.

Shuga knew he must choose his words carefully — very carefully — but his mind raced with a sudden apprehension.

"I was thinking," he began, "that when the *Official History* was recorded, New Yogo was just a newly formed country. Those who wrote it might have omitted facts that could make the people uneasy or cause unrest. If this letter is correct, not one but two creatures appear every hundred years: an egg and an Egg Eater. Not only that, but the sacred founder, Torugaru, and the first Master Star Reader joined forces with the Yakoo to kill the Egg Eater in order to protect the egg. The egg has some relation to water, and if it is not protected, a drought occurs. Which means that the Egg Eater is actually the demon — and it's the egg, not the demon, that's inside the Second Prince! If only we had known this sooner!"

The Master Star Reader did not respond. Looking at his face, Shuga feared that he had said too much. In his distress, he had unintentionally criticized the Master Star Reader's ignorance. Although he regretted his thoughtlessness, it occurred to him that if the Master Star Reader was angered by something like this, he was not worthy of his respect.

"Shuga." The Master Star Reader spoke at last. His voice was cold but it held no trace of anger. "People may discover and learn many things over time, yet they may also forget. The Star Palace has always had two sides. One is reading the future in the stars, to which we Star Readers have devoted our lives. The other is to guide this country's affairs aright.

"People always create problems, stirring up political intrigue. In every age, we Master Star Readers have been so busy running the country's affairs that we have little time left for Star Reading. Over time, we can come to see the world only from the viewpoint of politics. When I learned that something was inside the Second Prince, my first concern was how this would affect the government, even though I knew I should find out what the creature was." The hard edge had gradually left his voice. He stated objectively, without emotion, "The Hunters are not the only ones to blame. The first and gravest mistake was mine. I should have started by searching through the secret archives of the first Master Star Reader, Nanai."

"Secret archives?"

"Yes. In the Star Palace, there's a secret library, known only to the Master Star Reader, with the stone tablets on which Nanai recorded confidential information. But because the texts are written in ancient Yogoese, it takes a long time to decipher them.

"Shuga, I cannot search those records for clues now. It is my job to find a solution to the immediate political situation, which will take considerable time. Therefore, I must entrust this work to you. Make haste. Find out what happened two centuries ago."

Shuga bowed deeply. *The Master Star Reader is a wise man deserving of respect after all*, he thought with relief.

But the Master Star Reader was not finished. "Listen carefully, Shuga. We are not acting on the advice of that Yakoo magic weaver. We are doing this of our own accord. When you find the answer and everything has been resolved, this must be recorded in our history as the achievement of the Master Star Reader. You understand that, don't you? This is how the country is governed."

Shuga nodded. *Yes*, his heart whispered. *This is what must have happened two hundred years ago.*

The anxiety that had gripped him did not abate even after he left the room. It was not just their mistake in identifying the creature inside the prince or in dealing with it that bothered him. Until now, Tendo had been everything to him. He had believed that by mastering the knowledge of the Star Readers, he would some day reach the truth. Never had he doubted this. But now he wondered if it was really true. A disturbing thought stirred in the recesses of his mind: If the Yakoo magic weaver had known something that even the Master Star Reader did not, could other things affect this world besides Tendo?

C H A P T E R I V
THE LEGEND OF THE YAKOO

Balsa's wound healed even faster than Tanda had expected. "I'm lucky they didn't break any bones. Otherwise I would never have healed so quickly," Balsa murmured as Tanda removed the bandage to look at her wound.

He shook his head in mock disgust. The skin was already knitting together. "You get well so fast it's hard to believe that you're already thirty. But remember, you still don't heal as quickly as you used to. You're getting too old to push it." He pointed to her side. "Ah! I remember this one. I sewed you up that time too." He traced the scar tenderly with his finger.

Balsa pulled away from his touch. "Stop that! It tickles. You keep your hands off me." She grabbed the bandage from him and began to wrap it around the wound. Tanda drew back and rubbed his hands together. When the bandage was finished, Balsa stood up abruptly and went outside, keeping her face hidden.

Tanda sighed as he knelt beside the hearth to pick up the jar of ointment.

"Why are you sighing?" Chagum asked, looking into his face. He was trying to whittle a cooking skewer from bamboo — something Balsa had taught him to do — using a small knife he held awkwardly in his hands.

"If you don't keep your eyes on what you're doing, you'll cut yourself," Tanda said. He took the jar and placed it on a shelf, Chagum's eyes still following him.

"Tanda?"

"Mm."

"Why do you not marry Balsa? You get along so well."

Tanda looked slowly around at Chagum. "Don't ask me that," he said. "You shouldn't ask such things, you know."

"But —"

"Please, don't ask. Especially not when Balsa is here. Ever. Promise me."

Chagum looked as if he wanted to protest, but he said nothing. Tanda sat down beside him and said quietly, "There is something that Balsa has vowed to do. Her decision to become a bodyguard and her decision to risk her life in order to save yours is part of that vow. Until she fulfills it, I don't think that she will ever marry anyone."

"What is the vow?"

II4

"She vowed to save the lives of eight people."

"Why?"

"That's not for me to say. Someday you should ask Balsa. You're smart, so I'm sure you'll know when it's a good time. Ask her when she feels like sharing memories from her past." He smiled at Chagum and then went outside.

Balsa was standing beneath a tree, moving her arms and legs slowly as if drawing circles. Then she struck out suddenly with a jab and kick. "Ouch!" Her face twisted. She glanced at Tanda, who stood watching her with arms folded, and smiled wryly. "It still hurts a lot."

"What did you expect? Balsa, I'm going to Yashiro village. How about you?"

"You're going to find out about Nyunga Ro Im?"

"Yeah, I've asked around a bit and it seems that the person who knows most about it lives in Yashiro. Do you want to bring Chagum and come with me?"

Balsa shook her head. "I'll stay here. I'm a bit worried about letting other people see him, and I'm even more nervous about leaving him on his own. I thought I'd try teaching him some basic martial arts, a little at a time. That way he can at least protect himself in a pinch."

Tanda nodded. "All right, then. Help yourself to food from the storeroom when you're hungry. I may be a while, so don't worry if I don't make it back tonight."

Balsa nodded, but avoided his eyes.

The village to which Tanda hurried was a small community of about thirty people in the upper reaches of the Aoyumi River. Rice grew in the few fields along the river, while the terraced fields carved into the steep hillside were planted with various grains and vegetables. The villagers were a mixed race of Yakoo and Yogoese who lived in dome-shaped mud dwellings that looked like bowls turned upside down. Although such houses were traditional to the Yakoo way of life, their clothing, which consisted of a simple unlined jacket fastened with a wide belt over knee-length leggings, was typical of Yogo farmers. Some were dark-skinned like the Yakoo, while others were so fair they could not be distinguished from pure-blooded Yogoese. Yogoese was the common tongue, but, when startled, the elderly occasionally lapsed into Yakoo.

Tanda approached the Boundary Marker, a rope strung with bones that hung across the path between two wooden posts. As was the custom, when he passed beneath it, he brushed the top of his head against the bones to make them rattle. The Yakoo believed these bones had special powers of protection, and the rope kept evil spirits and demons from entering the village.

I wonder why they use nahji *bones*, Tanda thought idly. The *nahji* was a migratory bird that crossed the Misty Blue Mountains and flew over Yogo on its way to the sea at the midsummer solstice. This area didn't benefit from them in any way. Yet if one of these birds, exhausted from its flight, fell into the sea and was washed ashore, the Yakoo who lived along the coast would say special prayers for its soul, clean the bones, and sell them at the market. Yakoo from other parts of the country would pay a good price and take them home to use as charms.

Something stirred in the back of Tanda's mind, a distant childhood memory that he had not even known was there: his grandfather taking him by the hand as they walked beneath the *nahji* bones. Jealous of his grandfather, who was tall enough to make them rattle, the young Tanda had insisted that he be allowed to rattle them too. His grandfather had laughed and picked him up so his head could touch them, saying, "The *nahji* flies faster than the devil, faster than misfortune of any kind."

Tanda had begun to sing:

"Fly, nahji, *fly!*
Fly to the sea and make the rain fall;
make the rice grow tall."

"Ah, you remember well. That's the midsummer festival song. It's telling us that the rice we plant before the festival needs lots of rain to make it grow. I hope we have a good harvest this year too."

How old had he been? Tanda wondered. He walked along the mountain path lost in memory. Just then, the bushes in front of him rustled and out popped a little girl of about eleven years, carrying a basket filled with taro root. Water dripped from the basket, and the white skin of her cheeks and fingertips was flushed red.

"Oh, it's the healer!" She smiled up at him.

"Nina! Hello. You've been washing taro in the river, have you?"

"Yes." She fell in step beside Tanda. She looked so Yogoese that if she went to the city no one would suspect she had Yakoo blood in her. *If things go on like this, the Yakoo may disappear from the face of the earth before another century goes by*, Tanda thought.

"Where are you going?" she asked him.

"I want to ask your grandfather for some help. Can I carry that basket for you?"

"No, I can do it."

At the edge of the forest, they came to the village. The smell of wood smoke wafted toward them. The villagers' smiles were friendly, for at the turn of every season, Tanda brought herbs and medicines to each village in the area, and he always came to help when he heard someone was sick.

Tanda had timed his visit to coincide with the noon break, when the villagers returned from the fields, and he could see by the thin wisps of smoke rising from their houses that many were back already. Greeting people as he went, Tanda headed for a house near the mountain. Nina trotted along beside him, sometimes in front, sometimes behind. When they reached the house, she put her basket down with a thump beside the door and ran in shouting, "Grandpa, there's a guest to see you!"

As was tradition, Tanda wiped his feet twice on a little mound of earth in front of the entranceway to brush off bad luck. Only then did he enter the dim interior. The room was filled with the pungent smell of smoke. Woven straw mats covered the dirt floor, and the family was gathered around a fire pit in the center: Nina's grandfather, father, mother, and siblings.

"Hello, Noya," Tanda called.

The old man's eyes softened. "Why, if it isn't Tanda! It's been a while. Come in, come in. You've come at a good time — the taros are almost done. Sit and eat with us."

Tanda removed his straw sandals and came to sit beside the hearth. He drew a package of dried herbs from inside his tunic. "It's not much, but I brought some *todo*. I heard that your daughter-in-law here is pregnant, and this will help her morning sickness."

The young woman smiled shyly and murmured her thanks. She gestured to Nina to bring her the taros.

"Noya, there's something I wanted to ask you — in fact, it's why I came today. Your grandfather was a good friend of my great-great-grandfather's, right?"

"Yes, they were close friends. They often told me wonderful stories, but then your grandfather was given some fields in Toumi, where your grandmother was from. After he moved there, they didn't see much of each other."

"I actually came to ask about your father's older brother, the one who died when he was a child," Tanda said quietly. "About the Nyunga Ro Chaga, the Guardian of the Spirit — the Moribito."

Noya's face clouded, and he rubbed his chin with a gnarled hand. "Ah. Yes, my uncle was the Nyunga Ro Chaga. I heard about that. But, though they tried, our family couldn't protect him and the spirit's egg, and he died a horrible death. . . . It made my grandmother so sad whenever she thought of him that we just stopped talking about it. I'm sorry, I really don't know anything. If I did, you can be sure that I'd tell you."

Tanda's spirits sank. He should have expected this. It had been a terrible tragedy for Noya's family, and it was only natural that they would want to forget. Seeing the disappointment in his face, Noya said apologetically, "If you had come last year, when my mother was still living, it would have been different. She was the daughter of the village storyteller, and she knew a lot more than I did about my uncle and the Nyunga Ro Chaga, and spirits and things. . . . I was never really interested in all that. Besides, it happened so long ago — a hundred years now. Why do you want to know?"

For Tanda, this seemed the final blow: Even those who were related to the Guardian of the Spirit had forgotten the importance of this year, a century after his death. Just as he feared, the Yakoo were losing their lore with the years. *We've got to find Torogai,* he thought. *But can we do it in time?*

Suddenly there was a clatter as Nina dropped the taros and they rolled across the floor. She stood staring at the men with her mouth open. "Grandpa! Has it really been a hundred years since Nyunga Ro Chaga was killed!? But that's terrible! That means this is the year Nyunga Ro Im's egg will hatch!"

Everyone stared at her in amazement, but the most surprised of all was Tanda. "Nina, how did you know that?"

"I heard the story from my great-grandma," Nina said.

Noya hit his fist against his palm. "Why, of course! Nina was very attached to my mother — she was always badgering her to tell stories. Nina, what tale is this? Tell Tanda what she told you."

Nina blushed at the unexpected attention. "Nina, there's a good girl," Tanda said gently. "Come sit by me and tell me what you remember. Take your time."

She sat down beside him and, after squirming a little, began to speak. "Well . . . let's see . . . um, when grandfather's father's, um, older brother was, um, just a little boy, Nyunga Ro Im, the Water Guardian, laid an egg," she began. At first she stumbled over her words, but gradually she grew more relaxed and confident as the familiar phrases poured out. As he listened, it dawned on Tanda that fortune had smiled on him after all: Nina was telling him things that he had never known before.

"Nyunga Ro Im is born from an egg in the sea of Sagu, in this world. When it grows bigger, it swims up a river in

Nayugu, in the other world, and makes its home at the bottom of the deep, deep water. Once it's fully grown, it doesn't move. Great-grandma thought it became a huge shellfish. The energy it breathes out forms the clouds that cause the rain to fall in Nayugu as well as here in Sagu, and every hundred years it lays its egg and dies.

"After Nyunga Ro Im lays its egg, the clouds gradually disappear, and the sun beats down. To make sure the new Nyunga Ro Im is born and breathes clouds again, the Yakoo decided that they must help the egg. Since long, long ago, when the creatures of Sagu and Nayugu were still friends, they have done this. The spirit's guardian in this world, Nyunga Ro Chaga, nurtures the egg like a mother bird, protecting it until it is ready to hatch.

"But just as the snake seeks birds' eggs, so fearsome Rarunga, the Egg Eater, loves the eggs of Nyunga Ro Im and hunts them once they have been laid!" The little girl gave a violent shudder. "Great-grandma said that Grandpa's uncle was torn apart by the claws of Rarunga — torn in *half*! If a hundred years have passed, will Rarunga come to eat *us*?"

Tanda placed his hand on her shoulder. "Nina, it's all right. Rarunga only eats the eggs of Nyunga Ro Im. You can be sure he won't eat you, so don't be afraid."

Everyone's eyes were riveted to Tanda and the little girl. Even her mother had stopped in the middle of peeling more taros.

"Nina, about Rarunga, did your great-grandmother tell you anything at all about what kind of monster it was?"

"Yes, she said that her father saw it. They couldn't see anything until it ripped the Nyunga Ro Chaga in two, and then it just appeared! He remembered its big claws gleaming."

Then it is *a creature of Nayugu, not the Mikado's men*, Tanda thought. "Did she tell you if it had any weaknesses?" he asked her.

Nina shook her head sadly. "No. I asked her that too, because no matter how terrible the monster is, if you knew its weak point, you could kill it. But Great-grandma said that if they had known that, they wouldn't have let the boy be killed."

Tanda nodded. "That makes sense." He patted her shoulder. "Thank you, Nina. You've helped a lot. And it looks like you've inherited the storyteller's gift! I can see you're on the way to becoming a masterful storyteller, just like your great-grandmother."

Nina laughed happily, but on the other side of the hearth, Noya looked worried. "Tanda, I must ask you again: Why do you come to us now with these questions?"

Tanda looked at all of them and said, "I'm sure that you've already guessed; Nyunga Ro Im has laid its egg. And I want to protect it. But I beg you not to tell anyone what I've just said."

"Why?"

"The Mikado's sacred ancestor was supposed to have killed the Nyunga Ro Im, right? If word gets out that the Yakoo claim Nyunga Ro Im laid another egg, everyone who speaks of it will be beheaded as a traitor." The others exchanged shocked glances. "That's why it would be better not to mention this to anyone."

They nodded and placed the little fingers of their left hands to their lips in the Yakoo vow of silence. Tanda turned back to Nina. "You must promise too. Don't tell anyone, all right?"

She looked disappointed; she had clearly been planning to run and tell her friends all about it. Seeing the stern expression on her grandfather's and Tanda's faces, however, she made the vow of silence with her own little finger. Tanda smiled at her. Noya said solemnly, "Tanda, you must also vow to remain silent. Promise us you won't tell the authorities what we told you." Tanda nodded and made the sign. Then he stood up and bade them farewell, regretting that he left them in such a gloomy mood.

But as he passed through the door, Nina called after him. "Tanda, wait! I just remembered something! Something Great-grandma told me." He turned to look at her. Her eyes shone. "According to the legend, Rarunga doesn't come in winter. She thought it probably hibernates, like a mountain animal."

Her words seemed to have jogged Noya's memory, for he nodded and said, "She's right. My father's older brother was

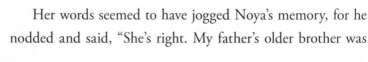

killed when it was almost midsummer. My grandmother always used to say how she wished that winter had never ended."

Tanda's heart leapt; this unexpected piece of information was priceless. He thanked them sincerely and, bowing low, left Noya's house. On his return, he passed quietly beneath the Boundary Marker, careful not to rattle the *nahji* bones. They swayed in the wind, which carried the faint scent of snow. It must already be snowing in Kanbal, Balsa's native land, which lay on the other side of the Misty Blue Mountains.

Looking up through the branches of the trees, he noticed that the red autumn leaves framing the cold gray sky were faded and sparse, exposing the bare branches. The signs of impending winter would normally have caused his spirits to sink, but right now he could only feel grateful. He walked along the mountain path, lost in thought.

CHAPTER V
REUNION WITH TOROGAI

Chagum was drenched in sweat. Balsa looked at him, her hands on her hips. "Are you tired?"

He nodded, unable to speak. After Tanda left, Balsa had begun teaching the boy some basic self-defense moves on the grassy space in front of the hut. The moves were the first forms of a martial art known as *chiki*, which she had learned at the age of six. Each movement was made in time to the rhythm of one's breathing — in, out, in, out, thrusting, striking, and kicking in slow motion. One hand struck while the other moved to protect a vital point, combining attack and defense in a single form, each designed to be practiced without a partner. After only twenty repetitions, Chagum was already gasping for breath.

"This will never do," Balsa said. "We'll have to build up your strength first. You're still a child and your bones aren't fully formed yet, so I don't want to push you too hard. But you'll have to at least get to the point where you don't run out of breath."

Chagum wiped the sweat from his eyes and winced. He hadn't known that sweat could sting so much. "How long must I practice before I become like you, Balsa?"

"Twenty years," Balsa answered calmly.

"Twenty years! That is impossible!"

"Chagum, you should say 'I'll never make it' or something like that to sound a little less regal. You don't want people to guess who you are every time you open your mouth, do you? As for not making it, a boy of your age with just a few months of training could never be a match for the kind of men who are after you."

"Then why should I bother — I mean, what's the point?" Chagum demanded indignantly.

"Simple. You'll have a better chance of escaping if you've practiced than if you haven't. Listen, Chagum. The tiniest thing can make a difference between life and death. If you can confuse your attacker for even one second, it just might give you the chance to get free. And an opening like that increases *my* chances of saving you. Believe me, it's better to have practiced than not," Balsa said. Suddenly she whipped around, her spear pointed toward the bushes. "Who's there?"

The bushes rustled and a monkeylike figure appeared. Balsa's eyes grew round with surprise. "Tor — Master Torogai!"

The magic weaver snorted. "What? You're here too? Looks like you're still reckless, lugging around that dangerous weapon as usual. And who's that kid?" Chagum was staring dumbfounded at this strange old woman dressed in tattered clothes. Her eyes narrowed suddenly. Without a word, she brushed past Balsa, stood squarely in front of him, and stared at him intently. They were almost the same height. When she placed her gnarled hand on his forehead, he shrank away from her. "Don't move!" she commanded, and he froze as if her words had gripped and bound him.

Barely touching him, her fingertips traveled from his forehead to his chest. The next moment, Chagum experienced a strange sensation: Her fingertips seemed to penetrate his clothes, his skin, even his muscles — to go right into his chest. He broke into a cold sweat; although the feeling was not painful, it was so strange he felt nauseated. Just when he thought he could bear it no longer, she removed her hand, and suddenly he was free. He crumpled to the ground like a puppet cut from its strings and sat there limply.

A thin sheen of sweat covered Torogai's brow. "Well, well," she muttered and, shaking her head slowly, turned to look at Balsa. "This must be what they call fate. The threads that tie us together in this world are strange indeed. Did the Second Queen hire you?"

Balsa nodded. There was no point in being surprised; Torogai was one of the sharpest people she had ever met.

"Master Torogai," she said. "I was looking for you. If this is fate, then for once I must be thankful for it."

Torogai grinned. "Me too. You've saved me a lot of trouble. But still —" She broke off for a second to look at Chagum, who had managed to get back on his feet. "A long life has its rewards. To think that I would live to see the egg of Nyunga Ro Im, the Water Guardian, with my own eyes."

Chagum's eyes widened. "You — You saw it? The thing inside my chest? Tell me what you saw. I command you to tell me!"

Torogai looked hard at him, then threw her head back and laughed. "Oho! Now I see. You're the Second Prince, are you? No wonder those hounds that came after me were so desperate." After she had had a good laugh, she turned back to him. "Your body is here in Sagu — because you are a creature of this world, you see. There's no egg embedded in your flesh or anything like that. I must say that I've never seen anything like it before: a creature of Nayugu superimposed on a creature of Sagu. What I saw was a small egg that glowed bluish-white. It doesn't have a hard shell; it's soft, like a fish egg."

Chagum grimaced. Despite her reassurance that it was not actually in his flesh, the idea was still repellent. He shook his head, struggling desperately to fight down his nausea. The magic weaver, however, paid no attention. "What did you do anyway?" she demanded. "How did you wind up with the egg?"

He glared at her. "I don't know. I remember nothing. I hoped that you would answer this question for me when we met. Why must I bear this spirit's egg?"

"You thought I would know? Well, boy, I hate to tell you, but there are some things that even I don't know! Hmm, too bad . . . I would love to learn how Nyunga Ro Im lays its eggs. Well, maybe you'll remember later — I guess I'll just have to wait. Hey, Balsa! Where's that dolt of an apprentice? Did you eat him?"

Balsa laughed. "I'm not so hungry as that! Tanda is —" she began and then turned to look behind her. A moment later, the bushes stirred and Tanda appeared, his hair covered in leaves. He stopped dead when he saw all three of them staring at him.

"What? What? Oh! Master Torogai! I've been looking for you!" His timing was so perfect that Balsa, Chagum, and Torogai looked at one another in disbelief.

"You know the saying, 'Speak of the sun and it shines'? Looks like there's some truth in that," Torogai said to Chagum with a grin. Then she turned to Tanda. "Look at your hair!" she yelled. "It's full of leaves! You'll never find a wife if you don't take care of how you look."

Tanda sighed. "You're covered in leaves too, and you have much more important work to do right now than worry about me finding a wife. Why don't we have some tea and something to eat while we talk?" He brushed the leaves from his hair and entered the hut.

They shared their adventures while sipping the aromatic tea that Tanda made. When they finished, Balsa said, "Let me get this straight. Nyunga Ro Im is some kind of spirit or creature that lives in deep water and breathes out clouds. Because it can't move by itself when it becomes an adult, once in a hundred years, just before it dies, it lays an egg in a creature of Sagu to be carried to the sea. If that's the case, then why don't we just hurry to the sea with the egg now?"

But Torogai shook her head. "No, I don't think that will work. It's not time yet. Chagum's dreams about water and the way he tries to walk into it are, I think, caused by the egg's memories of a time when it was in the water in Nayugu, and maybe it helps the egg get used to the water of Sagu. You said the water seemed thick and gluey, right? Perhaps as the egg matures it can change the water of Sagu like that. At any rate, I think that, when it's time, Chagum will start to move toward the sea without even thinking about it."

"Is it true that if the egg is protected until midsummer my life will be saved?" Chagum interrupted.

Torogai nodded. "I think so. Many years ago a creature of Nayugu told me that the egg laid by Nyunga Ro Im does not hurt its host."

Chagum looked relieved. Tanda placed a hand on his shoulder and smiled, but then turned to Torogai with a serious expression on his face. "But if it isn't protected, it will be eaten by Rarunga, right? Like a hundred years ago. Still, it's strange. I know there was a terrible drought at that time, but it didn't last a hundred years. Do you think Nyunga Ro Im really creates the clouds?"

Torogai shrugged her shoulders. "I don't know everything, you know. But if you think about it, there's a lot more to this world than the Nayoro Peninsula. Clouds form everywhere. Perhaps there is more than one Nyunga Ro Im. Or there may be more spirits that make clouds, just as there are many creatures that lay eggs — fish, birds, snakes. Some of the same creatures even lay their eggs in different ways.

"The one thing we know for sure is that here on Nayoro Peninsula, if Nyunga Ro Im's egg doesn't grow up and hatch, we get one heck of a drought. We have no choice but to protect that egg."

"I know," Tanda said. "And not just to save ourselves from drought. We must protect it because Chagum's life depends on it."

The conversation paused, and Tanda refilled everyone's cups. Chagum, his eyes on Torogai as she slurped her tea with relish, blurted out a question he had been longing to ask for some time. "Torogai, Tanda said I was the Moribito, the Guardian of the Spirit, because Nyunga Ro Im is a cloud spirit. But the masters at Star Palace taught me that a spirit is formed when the life forces of many things combine together, and that spirits are invisible beings with strange and mighty powers. Can something that is hatched from an egg and then lays eggs itself really be a spirit?"

Torogai looked up. "So that's what you Yogoese think, is it? Listen, boy. People from different countries who speak different languages have different ways of thinking. You know that, don't you? Take Balsa here. She's from Kanbal. The Kanbalese believe that thunder is a god. Right, Balsa?"

Balsa nodded. "That's right. In the beginning, the darkness created a whirlpool, and from it sprang the light. This was Yoram, the god of lightning."

Torogai returned her gaze to Chagum. "You see? You, Chagum, are Yogoese, and the Yogoese believe that their god is a giant formed when the world began through the merging of the most powerful life forces in the universe. When this god stirred the darkness, the heavens, which are lighter, rose above, while the earth, which is heavier, sank below. The earth gave birth to the goddess, and the goddess, together with the god, created the first human, the founder of your imperial line. Am I right?"

Chagum nodded. This story of the origins of his people was very sacred to him, and he stiffened, expecting the magic weaver to make fun of it. Seeing his expression, Torogai smiled suddenly. "Don't fret, boy. I'm not so foolish as to ridicule the myths and legends of other people. For countless generations, people, no matter where they're from, have been trying to understand this world of ours. The Yogoese believe in a giant god; the Yakoo believe that the first being was a swirling snake. How can I possibly say which is true? Nor is the Yogoese idea of spirits the same as the Yakoo idea. For us, spirits are things related to water, earth, fire, air, and wood that have great power. Take the trees growing in the mountains. A tree that has lived thousands of years comes to have great power, and we Yakoo think of it as a spirit. Even if it was just a little wee seedling thousands of years ago, we still call that tree a spirit."

"Great power? What kind of power?"

Torogai sighed. "Now listen here. It's not something that can be easily described in words. A tree spirit, for example, has a strong force, something like the power of life. That's what we call great power. As for Nyunga Ro Im, it can control water, breathe clouds, give birth to the rain. These great powers are what make it a spirit. . . . That's the kind of thing I mean."

Seeing the serious expression on Chagum's face as he pondered this, Balsa burst out laughing. "You look just like Tanda twenty years ago. Me, I find such abstract ideas impossible to follow. Do you like this kind of thing?"

Chagum thought for a moment and then said, "I wouldn't say that I like it. It's just that when I don't understand something, I have to think about it until I understand it clearly."

At this, Tanda smiled. "Chagum is more suited to being a scholar than a prince. Mind you, if princes were as thoughtless as Balsa here, the country would be in terrible shape."

"You can say what you like," Balsa snorted. "But getting back on topic, no matter what this Nyunga Ro Im is, we must protect Chagum from two things: Rarunga, the Egg Eater; and the Mikado's men."

Torogai scratched her chest roughly. "It will be much easier if those Star Reader fellows heed my message and mend their ways. Ah, but it makes me glad to know that that little girl in Yashiro village remembered the story of Nyunga Ro Im. If such little traces remain, there's hope yet."

"But I wonder why we lost that knowledge in the first place," Tanda said. "The story of Nyunga Ro Im is so important, it could save the country from famine. How could it vanish so easily from people's memories?"

Torogai glanced briefly at Chagum before answering. "I'm sorry to have to say this in front of the Second Prince, but I blame politics. The story of Nyunga Ro Im is directly tied to the legend of Torugaru founding this country. The Star Readers want to control everything in the universe, and therefore they can't let the people believe in the legends of the Yakoo. Yet, even so, some people still know them, like me and Noya's granddaughter. I learned the story of Nyunga Ro Im from my teacher, Gashin, and Tanda learned it from me. Unfortunately, our knowledge is incomplete. We lost the most important part of the story: how to destroy Rarunga. Yet some precious wisdom has still survived, like a thread slipping past the eyes of those who run the country."

Chagum frowned at Torogai. "Do the wise men in Star Palace truly manipulate the people the way you say? How would they do it?"

"By using things like the midsummer festival," Torogai replied.

At this the boy's eyes narrowed. "The midsummer festival is a festival celebrating our sacred ancestor's triumph over the water demon and the purification of this land. What about it?"

Torogai shook her head. "For the Yakoo, it was originally a festival to pray for a bountiful harvest. The Water Dwellers of Nayugu told me that midsummer's day is the day that Nyunga Ro Im will hatch its egg. I believe we passed on the knowledge of how that could be done safely through the midsummer festival. But now the festival has been changed into a celebration of Torugaru's victory. Even magic weavers like me have no way of knowing what the original festival was like or what knowledge has been lost. . . . That's the kind of thing I'm talking about."

Listening to their conversation, Tanda again felt a snatch of memory come unbidden to his mind: the festival song he had sung as a child when his grandfather let him rattle the *nahji*'s bones.

Fly, nahji, *fly!*
Fly to the sea and make the rain fall;
make the rice grow tall.

He remembered four wooden posts drenched in oil that were set ablaze on both banks of the river — how black they had burned; a play in which warriors used burning torches to fend off and corner a wildly dancing papier-mâché demon that was then slain by a hero; the sound of people singing an incantation to bring the blessed rain. Something tugged at his mind, but before he could grasp it clearly, Torogai began to talk again.

"I don't think those Star Readers could have forgotten something so important. The written word can be very powerful at times like this. If the way to beat Rarunga is preserved anywhere, it will be in their records. Of course, they've been so busy trying to run the country that they've forgotten their true purpose! It's been two hundred years, so insects might have chewed up all their books. . . . Even so, unless they are total fools, they'll realize something important is going on. They won't kill the prince if they don't have to."

"That's right," Balsa interjected. "Even when they attacked us, they weren't trying to kill Chagum." The boy looked at her in surprise. "That's why I was able to rescue you," she said, turning to him. "You didn't notice, but they had a perfect opportunity to kill you. If that had been their goal, they would have done it then. But instead, they changed their positions so they wouldn't hurt you and attacked me instead. I ran away from them so I could come back and rescue you when they split up and there was only one of them with you."

Chagum leaned forward eagerly. "That means, then, that my father — the Mikado — he's not trying to kill me?"

Balsa glanced quickly at Tanda. Before Torogai could open her mouth, he said, "Of course your father doesn't wish to kill you if he can avoid it. That would only be a last resort. But that doesn't mean you can relax. The Mikado is not an individual. He must think of the country first, of keeping it stable, before his feelings as a parent, so you must still be careful." He spoke with compassion, and Chagum accepted his words readily. "At any rate," Tanda added, "We can't go wrong if we prepare for the worst. I think we should move to the hunting cave early this year." Torogai and Tanda kept firewood, dried food, and other provisions in a cave deep in the mountains. Even in the midst of winter, when everything was buried in snow, they could live there without freezing to death.

In the end, they decided to leave the hut as soon as possible in order to make the cave livable before the snows came.

The next morning, while Tanda was off buying provisions in town, Balsa took Chagum to check the hunting traps. They spent the rest of the day smoking the fresh rabbit and

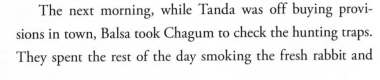

deer meat. Chagum hated skinning the rabbits; the worst of it was that they were still warm, which made them feel alive. He sobbed as he pulled the skin off the way Balsa showed him.

"The trick is not to think about it, Chagum. That will only make it worse. Move your hands without thinking." Balsa took her hunting knife and cut the outsides of the animal's leg joints, then snapped the bones in them one by one: *crack, crack.* She quickly sorted the entrails into those that were edible and those that were not, finished preparing their catch, and hung the meat in the smoke shack while it was still light. "If you smoke the meat," she told him, "it lasts much longer and tastes better too."

They continued working into the night. Balsa tanned the hides they had stripped from the animals and packed the smoked meat into bags. Tanda tied herbs into bunches or ground them into powder. Even Chagum helped, jumping up to do whatever he was asked. Torogai, however, did nothing. After supper, she drank the wine that Tanda bought her, then stretched out beside the hearth, the warmest spot in the room, and began to snore. Her face as she slept was the picture of happiness.

Within two days they finished packing. They closed up the hut and set off for the hunting cave, deep in the Misty Blue Mountains.

PART 3
MIDSUMMER'S DAY

CHAPTER I
WINTER AT THE HUNTING CAVE

Chagum had expected the hunting cave to be small, but when they reached it, he found it was far different from what he had imagined.

They had followed the Aoyumi River, climbing ever higher, until they passed beyond a waterfall and came to a grassy glade similar to the one in front of Tanda's hut. Behind this rose a gray cliff covered in a tangle of ivy and tree roots, which grew stoutly from any bit of soil lodged in the cliff's cracks or ledges and spiderwebbed across its face. Now, at the end of autumn when the signs of winter deepened, the trees had shed their leaves, exposing the gray stone in many places.

There was a small opening in the rock, just large enough for one person to stand in. Tanda lit a torch and entered. A moment later he called Chagum, who timidly stepped inside, then looked about in amazement. A cavern at least as large as the great hall in the palace lay before him. The ceiling was so high that the light of the torch did not reach it, nor could it penetrate the darkness at the cave's farthest end. He had expected the cave to be damp and dripping, but instead it was surprisingly dry.

"We call this the entranceway," Tanda said, his voice echoing hollowly. "It's too big, which makes it cold. Come this way, and I'll show you our home." Chagum hurried after him, with Balsa and Torogai not far behind. The torch illuminated three openings, one of which was covered by a wooden shutter. "You must never go into the cave on your right alone. It's very deep and has many branches. If you lose your way in there, you'll never get out again. The cave in the middle has a spring a little way inside with fresh, clean water. And the one on the left is the door to our house."

Tanda removed the shutter with a clatter and went inside. Chagum noticed a faint light farther in. A few steps through the door, the cave opened up into a wide space that made him gasp in astonishment. The walls of the oval chamber were smooth and dry. On the left wall near the ceiling, three smoke holes allowed the sunlight to pour through. Sturdy split logs covered the floor, with woven rush mats laid over them. A hearth was cut into the middle of the floor, and at the far end of the room, three large earthen jars and shelves lined with various pots stood testament to the cave's long use.

There was even bedding, wrapped carefully in oiled paper to keep it from getting damp.

"It looks so comfortable!" Chagum exclaimed.

"Of course! It's where we hibernate in winter. Give me a hand, will you? The bedding needs airing, and we have lots of cleaning to do."

For two days they worked hard to prepare for the long winter. On the morning of the third day, when most of the work was done, Torogai headed off with Tanda to Shigumano Canyon, where she hoped to meet the Juchi Ro Gai, the Mud Dwellers of Nayugu, and learn more about Rarunga.

"We ought to get there before the snow falls," she announced. "The Juchi Ro Gai might have already started their long winter sleep, but I suppose it's worth a try. Balsa, you take good care of that egg."

To Chagum's annoyance, she made it sound as if only the egg mattered. Seeing his expression, Tanda laughed. "Don't waste your time being angry. That's how she gets her kicks — making people mad — so don't give her the pleasure. Balsa," he added, "you take care."

Balsa folded her arms and raised her eyebrows. "Right, and what about you? Are you sure you can make it back before the snows come?"

"I don't know, but we'll be all right."

When they had left, the place seemed suddenly quiet. Chagum looked up at Balsa. "It feels lonely somehow."

"That's because they're so noisy! But we have so much to keep us busy that we won't have time to be lonely." She smiled. "And first, I've got to toughen you up."

Chagum's face fell.

In the days that followed, Balsa put the former prince through hours of *chiki* moves and many long runs through the forest. She also worked on improving his balance and taught him how to fall. Although Balsa was a strict teacher, she did not push him beyond his capacity, nor did she urge him on with praise or encouragement. Her approach was very matter-of-fact. The time flew by. Although Balsa remained alert for any sign of the Mikado's men, she saw none, nor did she sense any hint of Rarunga, that fearsome Egg Eater of Nayugu. They were busy with training and daily chores from dawn to dusk.

Sometimes when Chagum wandered through the forest, where the birds warbled sweetly, or when he sat by the hearth with Balsa in the evening, he felt disoriented, as though his previous life had been some strange illusion. Only a month had passed, but his life in the Second Palace seemed very long ago. He no longer dreamed about wanting to "go home" to some unknown place, and many days went by where he did not even feel like he was carrying the spirit's egg — as long as he did not remember why he was living in the cave with Balsa.

He fell into the habit of thinking in the late afternoons,

while he gathered firewood alone in the forest. As the rays of the westerly sun shone through the branches, his mind always returned to the same question. *Why me? Out of all the people in the world, why was I chosen to carry the egg?*

His first thought was that he had been chosen because he was a prince. But if that were true, then what about the Yakoo boy in the legend of Torugaru, and Noya's uncle a hundred years ago? They were commoners, and Yakoo. And besides, he was not a prince anymore. Every time he remembered this, his heart ached and he was overcome by a strange feeling. In the past, he had never questioned the fact that he was a prince; like the fact that he was the child of his mother and father, it seemed like something that would never change. Yet look how easily he had lost that rank and privilege! A person's fortune could turn at any time.

Oddly enough, he rather liked this new self, this boy who was collecting firewood. In fact, when he thought about the old Chagum, the prince who had never dressed or even washed himself because someone else always did it for him, he wondered what on earth he could have been thinking. At first, he had not even been able to tie a knot around the kindling he gathered every day. Now his hands deftly wound the string around the bundle and secured it tightly.

Not bad, he thought. Then he smiled. *I like being able to do things for myself. It's boring to do only what others tell you to. I don't want to be trapped as a prince anymore.* He swung the bundle of firewood onto his back and glanced up at the sky, with its clouds dyed red. A shadow crossed his face. *But now*, he thought, *I'm trapped as the Moribito, the Guardian of the Spirit.*

He had chosen neither role. He had never asked to be born a prince and certainly not to be the Moribito. Filled with a futile, choking anger, he came full circle back to his original question: *Why me?*

On the tenth day after Tanda and Torogai left, with a sound like a sigh, it began to snow. It fell thick and fast, burying the earth and the trees. Chagum helped wash up after dinner. That night, he put his hands out to warm them at the fire, only to draw them back hastily. For the first time in his life, they had become chapped, and the heat made them sting.

Balsa took his hands in hers. "Let me see. My! Just look at that chapped skin!" Chuckling, she rose and began rummaging among the things on the shelf. Finally, she returned with an ointment that she rubbed into his cracked fingers. Chagum looked at her hands as they worked. They were so different from his mother's — thick and rough and covered in calluses from wielding the spear. But when he felt their warm, dry touch, tears welled unbidden and spilled down his cheeks.

Balsa said nothing, but simply kept rubbing his hands. The blizzard raged outside, but the cave under the snow was warm and silent, as if they were in the bowels of the earth.

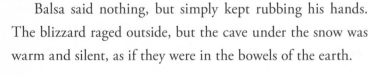

"I hate snow," Chagum whispered. "It swallows up sound, and I feel like I can't breathe."

Balsa patted his hands lightly and let them fall. "Then how about I tell you a story to help you?" she said.

Chagum's face brightened instantly. "What kind of story?"

"The story of a country far to the north, and of a little girl who was the daughter of the king's physician." Staring into the crackling flames, she began. "If you travel across the Misty Blue Mountains and keep going north, farther and farther, you will come to a country called Kanbal. Unlike your country, Kanbal doesn't have good fields — only mountains covered year-round in snow, and some steep, rocky slopes. The people survive by planting tough grains and potatoes and raising goats on the mountainsides. The huge eagles that live on the cliffs feed on mice and goats, or other animals that fall to their deaths. . . . They especially love the marrow inside the bones, and they'll drop them from great heights to crack the bones open and get the marrow. I can still hear the sound of the bones hitting the rocks, echoing in the valley — *crack, crack*. That's what Kanbal, my homeland, is like.

"Although it was a poor country, the old king had several wives and many children — four princes and five princesses. When the princes grew up, they began to fight over who would be the next king, as princes often do. Rogsam, the king's second son, was a particularly evil man. When his

149

father died, Rogsam made sure that his older brother Naguru was set on the throne. Then he poisoned Naguru before he could have any children.

"No one guessed that the new king had been murdered. He had always been sickly, and everyone in the palace knew he had caught a bad cold that winter. They thought he just died of it.

"But there was one man who knew Rogsam's secret — - Naguru's physician, Karuna Yonsa. Rogsam had ordered him to poison the king and threatened to kill his daughter if he didn't obey. Karuna's wife had died the year before, so this daughter was all he had left in the world. He knew that Rogsam was a cruel man, not above murdering a little girl. So in order to save her, Karuna did as he was told and poisoned the king.

"But then he knew too much. He was sure that once the king was dead, Rogsam would never let him or his daughter live. So he secretly asked his good friend Jiguro Musa to take his daughter and run away with her as soon as the king died. Jiguro was Rogsam's martial arts instructor, and saving Karuna's daughter would mean the end of the life he knew. You can see that, can't you? To escape with the girl, he would have to give up everything — his position in the palace, his whole life. Rogsam would never let him get away once he realized that he knew the secret of the king's death.

"And yet Jiguro accepted his friend's request." Balsa's eyes were tinged with sorrow. "He and the little girl ran away into hiding. Rogsam sent warriors to kill them, and Jiguro fought them one by one. And again and again, he took the girl and fled.

"Soon they heard that Karuna had been killed by thieves. The girl felt as though her heart had been cut in two. She hated Rogsam. She vowed that one day, she would rip him to pieces with her own two hands. She begged Jiguro to teach her how to fight.

"At first, he refused. Martial arts were for men, he insisted. Girls didn't have the strength for it. But the real reason he refused to teach her was because he didn't want her to live a life of bloodshed. It's strange, but once you learn to fight, you seem to attract enemies. . . . Sooner or later, those who master the art of combat must end up fighting.

"In the end, however, Jiguro gave in, for two reasons. One was so that she could escape and survive on her own if he was killed by their pursuers. The other was because he recognized that she was born with natural talent."

"What kind of talent do you need for martial arts?" Chagum asked.

"Many different kinds. This girl could mimic a move perfectly after seeing it only once. She could also —" She broke off and held up her index finger. "Chagum, can you hit the same spot over and over again with your finger?"

He gave it a try, tapping his fingertip against a charred spot on the edge of the hearth. It was surprisingly difficult; the faster he tried to hit it, the more his finger wavered and missed the spot. Balsa suddenly began tapping a much smaller spot right beside his. Her finger moved so fast it looked blurred, and though she was hitting the point from a greater distance, she always touched the same place, as though drawn to it by a magnet.

She stopped and said, "The little girl had always been good at that. And she had other abilities — she was light on her feet and more aggressive than most boys. Jiguro decided that she was born to be a warrior, that it was her destiny to master the martial arts.

"Their journey continued, with Jiguro teaching her as they went. One or two years passed. Sometimes they had to do dirty work just to make enough to eat. Jiguro was hired as a bouncer for a gambling den. The girl ran errands and even begged. That's how they survived. They could never stay in one place for long because their enemies might find them. And no matter how careful they were, in the end, the enemies always did find them." The sadness in her eyes deepened. "Jiguro was so strong, Chagum. None of his attackers could beat him. But the little girl knew that every time he killed one of them, it broke his heart. For you see, they were all his old friends — the people he had trained with long ago. I don't think they wanted to fight him either, but if they disobeyed the king, they would be killed and so would their families. So they came to kill Jiguro, their hearts in agony.

"Eight men he killed, eight friends, to protect himself and the girl, and this lasted fifteen years. Then Rogsam died of a sudden illness, his son became king, and there was no longer any need to hide. Those fifteen years were hell, Chagum. By then, the six-year-old girl had become a young woman of twenty-one. She was warrior enough to beat Jiguro one out of every two tries."

The logs in the fire had died down to embers. A silence filled the dimly lit cave.

"That girl was you, wasn't it?" Chagum asked.

"Yes."

"And that's why you vowed to save the lives of eight people. The same number that Jiguro had to kill to save you," he said hesitantly.

Balsa looked at him in surprise. "Tanda must have told you that. So you knew that story already?"

Chagum shook his head. "No. When I asked him why he didn't marry you, he said you had made a vow to save the lives of eight people, and until you'd done that, he didn't think you would marry anyone. That's all."

Balsa sighed. Then she laughed wryly but said nothing. Her face was etched with a startling loneliness.

To his surprise, Chagum found himself pitying her, from the very bottom of his heart. Balsa seemed invincible, endowed with powers no other warrior could match, but in her profile he could glimpse the shadow of a young girl, hurt and buffeted by a cruel and hopeless fate. If he had never experienced what it was like to be at the mercy of fate himself, he would not have noticed, but now he could see it with unbearable, heartrending clarity. A warm tenderness welled up inside him. He wanted to say something but could not think of anything. All he could whisper was, "Balsa, what number am I?"

She laughed but did not answer. Instead, she wrapped her arms around him and hugged him tightly. "When Jiguro was dying," she said, "I told him to rest easy because I would atone for the wrongs my father committed. 'I'll save the lives of eight men,' I told him. But, you know, he just smiled. 'It's much harder to help people than to kill them,' he told me. 'Don't be so hard on yourself, Balsa.'

"He was right. If you want to save someone in the middle of a fight, you can only do it by hurting someone else. While saving one person, you earn yourself two or three enemies. After a while, it becomes impossible to figure out how many people you've really saved. Now, Chagum, I'm just living."

The blizzard blew for two days, finally ceasing at dawn on the third day. The sky was clear and the snow shone so brightly it hurt the eyes. A little past noon, Tanda returned, tramping through the freshly fallen snow.

"Where's Torogai?" Balsa asked.

Tanda grinned. "She said she didn't want to spend the winter holed up in the mountains. But there are too many eyes in the city, so she'll stay at the hot spring in Tangaru. She'll be back when the snow melts."

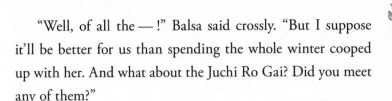

"Well, of all the — !" Balsa said crossly. "But I suppose it'll be better for us than spending the whole winter cooped up with her. And what about the Juchi Ro Gai? Did you meet any of them?"

"Not one. It was a waste of time. Nobody responded to us at all. I don't know if it was because they were already asleep for the winter, or if they just didn't want to tell us about Rarunga. After all, it lives in the earth of Nayugu, just like them. We'll have to try again in the spring."

Sitting at the hearth sipping his tea, Tanda smiled suddenly.

"What are you grinning about?" Balsa demanded.

He just shook his head. He was afraid she might run away again if he told her how glad he was to be spending the winter with her in the cave.

C H A P T E R   I I
IN THE SECRET ARCHIVES

It was an unforgettable winter for Shuga as well. The Master Star Reader gave him the key to the secret archives and relieved him of all other duties and training, and he immersed himself in deciphering Kainan Nanai's memoirs, which had lain undisturbed for almost two centuries.

A few air vents provided the only openings in the underground archives, and no light entered from outside. Shuga brought ten fat candles and used mirrors to reflect their light. Although he would have liked to bring down a charcoal brazier for warmth, he had been warned that burning charcoal in that small space could poison him. The room was freezing, but he wore padded clothing and relied on the faint warmth of the candles for heat.

He only left the archives twice a day, for breakfast and supper, and whenever he entered the dining hall, he had to endure the cold stares of his fellow Star Readers, who pointedly ignored him. The hatch that opened into the archives was located in the Master's stone-tiled room, and as a result, everyone else believed that Shuga was working for the Master Star Reader on some special task. *People are so petty*, he thought frequently. How could these men, who had supposedly chosen the study of Tendo as their life's work, waste their time envying his success? Would he do the same, he wondered, if he were in their position? He thought not, but he supposed it was possible he might feel very jealous. Whichever the case, he did not let such a little thing discourage him. The more he read, the more engrossed in the memoirs he became. The content was so fascinating that he often forgot to eat supper.

Nanai's memoirs were carved onto stone tablets, each crammed with fine script. He had probably originally written them in ink on cloth or hide, but his successors had spent much time and effort copying them onto stone so they would not disintegrate over the years. It must have been a daunting task, for his memoirs amounted to several hundred stone tablets. They began with Nanai's memories of his youth, when he spent his days studying Tendo, being trained to read the future in the stars. He recorded everything in scrupulous detail, and as Shuga read, it gradually dawned on him why Nanai had been so meticulous about recording events: He knew that time will always twist the truth and facts will always be changed to embellish a story or create a myth. Nanai realized that he would be the main character in the story of New Yogo's founding. Therefore, in addition to the distorted facts that eventually became legend, he secretly recorded what he had really experienced for future generations.

Reading further, Shuga also began to see why this record had to be kept secret. The first Mikado, Torugaru, had been a weak and cowardly man without a mind of his own. It was not because he had tired of the pointless conflict in his home country that he renounced his right to the throne, but because he was afraid of being killed. Nanai had chosen him for this very weakness, for his docility: He was easy to manipulate, a puppet in king's clothing.

It was the tales he heard from a Star Reader and explorer that drew Nanai to the Nayoro Peninsula. According to the explorer, it was a very rich land, easy to protect from enemy attack. He had also been impressed by the Yakoo belief that the visible and invisible worlds of Sagu and Nayugu intertwined to create a vibrant universe. Nanai was terribly disappointed that the Yakoo fled into the mountains when the Yogoese reached the peninsula, as he wanted to question them and learn more. But he had no time to seek them out; he had to make the incompetent Mikado establish a new country. Comments such as *I wish he'd use his own brains once in a while!* peppered his memoirs, and Shuga found himself liking the man, who indulged in a little grumbling as he poured his heart and soul into his tremendous task.

The memoirs were written in ancient Yogoese, which was

very difficult to read. By the time Shuga reached the point where Nanai had founded the nation, winter was coming to an end and the new year had already begun. Although he was unaware of it, there had been much less snow than usual, and the Star Readers confirmed the coming of a terrible drought.

While Shuga remained secluded in the archives, a great change had taken place within the palace. The Mikado's first-born son, fourteen-year-old Sagum, had caught a cold early that winter, and he was now deathly ill. The Master Star Reader stayed closeted with the prince's physician in Ichinomiya Palace for days on end, trying desperately to save the boy's life.

Sagum and Chagum were the Mikado's only sons; the Third Queen had as yet only given him daughters. The Mikado privately consulted the Master Star Reader about his gravest fear. "Sagum may die," he said in an anguished voice. "Should that happen, what am I to do about Chagum?" Chagum was, after all, his son. They might not live under the same roof the way commoners did, but he still loved him. He had tried so hard to live up to his role as ruler that, when he had learned that his second son harbored the water demon, he had steeled himself to sever any attachment to him — ordering his death, because that is what a Mikado must do. But once the heat of the moment had passed, Chagum's face had begun to haunt him.

"Mikado," the Master Star Reader said. "Haste is dangerous. Do not worry. There are many possible ways to handle
this, depending on how things develop. Our first priority
must be to heal Prince Sagum. In the meantime, I will order
the Hunters to find Prince Chagum as quickly as possible
and bring him safely back to you." With these words, he
calmed the Mikado's fears.

He left the Mikado's presence, and as he walked toward
the Star Palace, he happened to glance up at the sky. Stars
were scattered like sand across the firmament in a breathtaking display. He felt something akin to pain stir in the depths
of his heart. *It has been so long since I read the stars. To think
that a Star Reader should have no time for that!* He was no
longer a Star Reader, he thought, not in the true sense of
the job.

He resumed walking, following his servant, who carried
a lantern to light their way. *Instead of a Star Reader, I've
become a lantern bearer, lighting the path this country will take.*
He was suddenly acutely aware of the heavy burden of
responsibility he bore, and with it, a great fatigue, something
he had been too busy to notice for a long time.

When he reached his chamber, Gakai was already there
waiting for him. "Have you prepared the statement to the
people about the impending drought?" the Master Star
Reader asked him.

Gakai nodded. "Here is the message that will be given to
every village chief," he said.

The Master Star Reader took the paper from him, but the expression on his face grew stern as he read it. He raised his head abruptly, his keen eyes fixed on Gakai. "This is not what I told you. My orders were to reduce the percentage of rice planted to one-fifth, and to plant tougher crops like *shiga* and *yassha* instead. But you've written that they should plant one-third of their fields with rice. Why did you change it without asking me?"

A thin film of sweat shone on Gakai's forehead, but he returned the Master Star Reader's gaze steadily. "I apologize for acting on my own. But the Chief Treasurer strongly objected to cutting rice production to one-fifth. He insisted that it would ruin the country."

Rice was the country's most valuable crop because the people paid their taxes with it. It was collected from each village and then brought to the country's storehouses, from which a certain amount was sold to merchants for cash. It was only natural that the Chief Treasurer, who was responsible for the nation's coffers, would violently object to reducing rice production, and the Master Star Reader had fully expected his interference. He breathed a mental sigh. Gakai would obviously never be suited to serve as the Master Star Reader. "Of course the Chief Treasurer complained," he said. "That's his job — to protect the government's wealth. But why did you, a Star Reader, do what he said without question?"

Gakai looked perplexed. "Because . . . I thought that

protecting the country is the most important thing for Star Readers too."

The Master Star Reader shook his head slowly. "What on earth have you learned in all the time you've been in the Star Palace? You've spent your days studying the majestic truth that all those who live on this earth are inextricably bound to the stars in the heavens, moved by invisible threads — yet you still don't understand how this country works! Anyone involved in the political affairs of this land, not just the Chief Treasurer, is going to put the nation's wealth first, especially the government officials who skim profits off the merchants. To them, the death of one or two hundred peasants from starvation is far preferable to reducing the amount of money in the treasury. This is precisely why we need Star Readers. We can see much farther into the future than anyone else, with much broader vision. It is this that enables us to lead the country properly.

"Can't you see? If we make the farmers plant rice because of our greed, in the fall we will reap only withered crops and the bitter anger of people dying from starvation. And that anger will run deep and swell until it shakes the country to its foundations." Gakai stared at the ground. The Master Star Reader's voice was quiet but firm, brooking no further argument. "Rewrite the message and make sure it reaches every chief in the land as quickly as possible. Do you understand?"

Gakai could only nod his head.

CHAPTER III
THE CHANGE BEGINS

About four months after they had moved to the hunting cave, when the snow on the mountains was finally beginning to melt, an odd change came over Chagum.

"Hey, Chagum, are you planning to sleep all day?" Balsa scolded him as she started to pull off his quilt.

He looked up at her, drowsy-eyed. "Balsa, I'm tired. My body feels so heavy."

She placed her hand on his forehead and inclined her head to one side. "Maybe you've caught a cold. You don't seem to have a fever, though. Tanda, can you come here a minute?" she asked, turning toward him. He looked up from the fire, where he was putting water on to boil. "Chagum says he's not feeling well."

Tanda knelt down beside him. He told him to stick out his tongue, then felt below his ears. Next, he picked up his

slender wrist and checked his pulse. He sat for a while counting and then said, "Hmm, his pulse is a bit slow. Chagum,
do you notice any other difference besides the fact that you
feel tired?"

"I'm sleepy . . . I feel as if . . . I'm being pulled . . . to the
bottom . . . of . . . the . . . earth." His eyes closed and he fell
fast asleep. Tanda and Balsa looked at one another.

"Do you think the egg is doing this?"

"Well, the symptoms are a little strange for a cold. It will
soon be spring. Maybe the egg is starting to grow. That could
cause changes in his body."

"What should we do? Should we wake him up? What if
he never wakes up?!"

"Calm down, Balsa. If this is the work of Nyunga Ro Im,
it shouldn't hurt Chagum. If it's Rarunga, then we ought to
feel something, but I can't sense any danger. Can you?"

Balsa probed with her mind for some other presence near
Chagum. "No, I don't sense any danger or hostility. But
remember, Rarunga is not human. Maybe my intuition won't
sense something from an invisible world like Nayugu."

"I doubt it. Chagum lives in Sagu. Even if the monster's
home is in Nayugu, it will have to appear in this world to
attack him. A hundred years ago, they saw the claws that
ripped the child apart, remember? I'm sure we'd notice something if it was going to show up here. Whatever the case, I
should probably take a look inside him."

He rubbed his palms together, half closed his eyes, and

began muttering under his breath. Then he pulled back the covers and laid his hands on Chagum's chest. Balsa, watching with bated breath, noticed that his hands seemed blurred. Looking closely, she saw that Chagum's chest was also beginning to blur — and then suddenly they seemed to merge together. Tanda pulled his hands away abruptly and gasped for air, like someone surfacing from underwater.

"Are you all right?" Balsa asked, peering at him with concern.

Tanda waved a hand in front of his face. "Phew! That was exhausting!" He keeled over backward and lay on the floor, covering his face with his hands. Once he had caught his breath again, he sat up. "It's just as I thought. The egg is changing. It's much bigger, so big that I can see something pulsing inside it."

Balsa frowned. "Are you sure Chagum will be all right? Even with some other creature growing inside him? Digger wasp larvae eat their host when they hatch. . . . You don't think this creature will consume Chagum, do you?"

Tanda brushed the hair from his forehead where it clung, damp with sweat, and shook his head. "No, I don't think so. Here in Sagu, Chagum's body has not really been weakened at all."

"But just look at him! He was so tired he fell asleep again."

"I think those are just signs that his body is trying to adjust naturally to the growth of the egg. You saw how wiped out I was just now, didn't you? Even with training as a magic weaver, it's grueling to span the worlds of Sagu and Nayugu. Up to now, Chagum hasn't seemed tired at all, even though he is constantly straddling two worlds. This must mean that his body has already adjusted to it. But now the egg is growing and entering a new stage. Adjusting to this change probably requires a lot of energy. I think he's sleeping to conserve his strength."

Seeing her dubious expression, Tanda smiled. "You don't believe me, do you? Because it's me, right? But Torogai said the same thing. We don't know how Nyunga Ro Im lays its egg in someone from Sagu, or how it chooses that person. But look around at this world, how perfectly it's made. Flowers can't move, yet the insects come to them and spread their pollen. Trees can't move either, but birds and animals eat their fruit and carry their seeds far and wide. There must be something about Chagum that makes him suitable for the job of carrying the egg. Torogai only shares a tenth of what she knows, but if she felt there was any danger, she would have told me. Don't worry. It'll be all right."

Balsa looked keenly at him; he showed no trace of anxiety. "You seem very calm about it," she said.

"Really? I guess I was expecting something like this to happen. Come on. Let's have breakfast. After all, we have no choice but to let things take their course."

Balsa sighed and did as he suggested. But despite what he had said, the dark cloud of anxiety that weighed on her mind did not disappear. Tanda and Torogai were magic weavers; they had kept company with spirits and the supernatural all their lives. But she had not, and therefore she found it hard to believe that this cloud-puffing spirit, Nyunga Ro Im, would not harm Chagum.

They made hot rice porridge over the hearth, adding a little salt for flavor, and had begun eating when Tanda noticed Balsa staring vacantly into the flames.

"Balsa."

"Hmm?"

"You look so depressed. What are you thinking about?"

"Nothing . . . Just that winter's almost over."

"It was a good winter, wasn't it? Just the three of us, working and relaxing together. Like Noya's grandmother, I wish this particular winter would never end. But spring is coming."

"And then we'll say good-bye to peace and quiet. Rarunga will wake, and it will be do or die."

Tanda gazed at her. "You're right. From now on, we'll be fighting for our very lives." Then he added, "If we survive, why don't we stay together, the three of us, just like we did this winter?"

Balsa's eyes wavered. Tanda said quietly, "I've been waiting all this time. You know that. I thought I would wait until you had fulfilled your vow." His eyes suddenly filled with something that could have been either sorrow or anger. "But I've begun to think maybe you'll never come back, no matter how long I wait. Your life has become one long, bloody battle. Somewhere along the line you started to fight just for the sake of fighting."

Balsa did not answer, but in her heart she knew that he was right. The fighting impulse had penetrated the very marrow of her bones. During the winter, there had been times when she had been burning for a fight. She smiled wryly. "What should I do? Do you have any medicine that can cure me?"

Tanda smiled bleakly and shook his head. "If you can't believe *I* could be that medicine, then there's no point in waiting, is there?" Without another word, he stood up and went outside.

Balsa sat staring at the porridge bubbling in the pot over the fire. A heavy sadness simmered inside her. For an instant, she thought of running after him and grabbing his arm, but she did not. She closed her eyes and rubbed her face with her hand. *Idiot! How could he distract me at a time like this?!* She felt hot tears welling up but sat motionless, with her eyes closed.

Where he went she did not know, but Tanda did not come back even in the afternoon. Balsa spent the day working silently. It was sunset by the time Chagum finally woke. She was just coming in with a bundle of firewood when he opened his eyes with a groan.

"Chagum? How do you feel?"

He stared at her with unseeing eyes for a moment, then murmured, "It seems so dark, Balsa."

"That's because the sun's already setting. You spent the whole day sleeping, you know. Do you still feel tired?"

He shook his head and sat up. "I'm thirsty," he said hoarsely. Balsa brought him some water in a bowl and he gulped it down noisily.

"Are you all right?"

"Yes, but my head feels kind of fuzzy."

"That's because you slept so long. If you're feeling all right, go outside and get a bit of fresh air. That should wake you up." Chagum nodded and stood up. He changed into his clothes slowly and went outside. Just as Balsa was moving the ashes in the hearth to one side to lay new logs on the fire, she heard him scream.

Grabbing her spear, she raced outside, but she could detect no sign of an enemy or even anything out of the ordinary. All she could see was Chagum's dark silhouette at the cave's entrance, outlined in the bright rays of the setting sun. His hands were clamped over his mouth, and his body was rigid and shaking violently. He was as taut as a fine string stretched to breaking point.

"Chagum! What's wrong?"

He turned, his eyes rolling and his face contorted in sheer terror. She grabbed him and pulled him to her, hugging him tightly. There was nothing to scare him, nor could

she sense any invisible presence. Yet something was not right. Chagum's small frame seemed insubstantial, as if he would vanish from her arms at any moment, and Balsa felt dizzy, though she could not understand why. She blinked. The scenery around her looked blurred and dim, as if it were wavering.

"Balsa!" A voice thundered in the core of her being. She recognized it as Tanda's, but it was filled with a powerful intensity that she had never heard from him before. "Chagum is being pulled into Nayugu. Don't let yourself be dragged in with him. Center your energy in the pit of your stomach. Be like a pillar, grounding him in Sagu. Balsa!"

She took a long, deep breath and concentrated her energy in her center. A warm ball of power formed inside her, calming her, and the dizziness passed. Chagum let out a thin whistle of breath followed by a high-pitched wail: "Help! I'm going to fall! I'm going to fall!"

"Chagum!" Tanda's voice reverberated like a huge drum through Chagum's body, beating heavy and deep. "Calm down. It's all right. What you see is only Nayugu, that's all."

"There's nothing under me! Just a deep valley —" Chagum began to scream, his eyes closed. Balsa tightened her hold, but he kept on screaming.

"Tanda! What should I do?"

The words had no sooner left her mouth than she felt two large, warm arms enfold them both. In a low voice, Tanda began chanting in Chagum's ear — no words, just sounds. Like the rhythmical murmur of waves washing against the shore, calming vibrations rolled from him to the boy. Chagum stopped screaming, and his shaking slowly lessened.

"Chagum, relax," Tanda said. "The valley you see is not where you are standing. You're looking at the land of Nayugu. Can you hear me? Your body is here, standing right on the ground of Sagu. It's all right. You won't fall." He gently let them go and stepped back. "Calm your mind and feel Balsa's arms around you. Can you feel them now?"

Chagum nodded. "Now use Balsa as a guide," Tanda continued. "Start from where you feel her arms around you. Feel your own body, slowly. Your arms, back, chest, stomach . . . now your legs. Can you feel your legs?" Again, Chagum nodded. "Now feel the ground under your feet. How about it? Can you feel it? The hard earth?"

Balsa felt Chagum gradually stop trembling. He had been standing on tiptoe, as if straining to drift away, but now he relaxed and his heels slowly returned to the ground. She felt him shift his weight onto his legs.

"Ta-Tanda, there's ground under my feet!"

"Of course. Bring your mind back here. Try to remember what this world looks like. You're standing at the entrance to the hunting cave where we've lived all winter." Chagum quietly opened his eyes. His face was beaded with sweat. "Can you see me?" Tanda asked.

He looked at Tanda. His gaze wavered but then gradually focused. "Yes, I can see you."

"It's all right. Don't worry. Nayugu pulled you in because it became visible to you so suddenly. But you'll be okay now. It's just like swimming: Once you know how, it's so easy you wonder why you had to struggle so much. Now that your mind is used to being able to see Nayugu, you should be able to control it so that you only see Sagu, if that's what you want. Try it and see. Can you do it?"

Chagum wiped the sweat from his face. "Yes." He heaved a large sigh, and beside him Balsa finally relaxed.

Tanda looked at her and said with feeling, "We're very lucky you were nearby when it happened. You've always been able to respond instantly to danger. I doubt any ordinary person could have centered herself so quickly. It was because he had you to cling to that he was saved. On his own, he might have lost his mind."

"I only managed it because you shouted at me," Balsa answered. "I had no idea you could do that! With that kind of power, you would have made a good warrior, if you'd just tried a little harder." She tried to smile.

He looked at her as if to say it was no joke, then he put his hand on Chagum's back and gently nudged him toward the cave. "You know," he said to Chagum, "when I looked at the egg this morning, it had grown quite a bit. That's probably why this happened. I'm guessing that this kind of thing will happen more often, so you'll need to learn how to calm your mind instead of panicking like you did just now. It could mean the difference between life and death."

Chagum pressed his lips tightly together and nodded. Sweat still covered his face. He swallowed once or twice, as though trying to keep himself from vomiting, and began to shake. Then suddenly a great cry burst from his lips. "It's not fair! It's not fair!" Tears flew from his eyes. "Damn it! Why? Why me? Why do I have to go through this? Stupid egg! Taking over my body! I wish it would just die!"

He struck out wildly, kicking the air and the cliff and tearing at his chest, until Balsa scooped him up from behind and flung him to the ground. Thrown into the grass, he rolled, then stood up and flew at her, yelling at the top of his lungs. She braced herself and once again he went sprawling on the ground. Again and again he flung himself at her, only to be thrown down. At last, when he could move no longer, he lay on his back in the grass where he had fallen, sobbing and gasping for breath. After some time, he sat up slowly and looked at Balsa. He was startled to see she was crying too. Without bothering to wipe away her tears, she silently took him by the arm and led him into the cave.

Tanda remained where he stood in front of the entrance. The sight he had just witnessed had brought an old memory vividly to his mind, a memory that stabbed his heart — Balsa as a young girl throwing herself, weeping and wailing, at Jiguro, who caught her and flung her head over heels to the ground. She must have felt just like Chagum did now: rage with no outlet; anger at the cruel fate she was forced to bear, at the life she had to lead. He paused suddenly in surprise. *Is that why Balsa can't stop fighting?* he wondered. *Is she unable to escape this cycle of bloodshed because she's still angry deep in her soul?*

He could not get the thought out of his mind. He waited until Chagum had fallen asleep and then, after some hesitation, he asked her about it. She smiled faintly as she listened. "Hmm. So you were thinking of Jiguro too," she murmured, staring at the flickering embers in the hearth. "Rage. Yes, it's true that there's always some anger smoldering inside me here," she said, rubbing her chest. "But when I was wrestling Chagum, I was thinking of something a little different. For the first time, I could understand how Jiguro must have felt when he caught me and threw me to the ground." She looked up at him suddenly and smiled. "I guess you wouldn't make a good warrior after all. Anger. You think that's the reason I can't leave bloodshed behind?" She sighed deeply. "I wish it was that simple. Tanda, the problem is that fighting is in my very bones. I don't have any fancy, noble reason like anger at my fate. I'm just like a gamecock that launches itself into battle after meaningless battle. I like fighting. That's why I can't stop."

From that day on, Chagum spent much of his time moping sullenly. He flared up angrily at the slightest thing, storming out of the cave and not returning until nightfall. Balsa and Tanda said nothing, just let him be.

One afternoon, Chagum came rambling back from gathering firewood with a few small sticks that barely passed for a bundle. Balsa was skinning a rabbit she had hung from a tree branch, and he noticed that the knife she was using was his dagger. Like a bent bamboo tree suddenly springing free, anger erupted inside him, a blind rage that not even he understood. He threw down the firewood, ran up to her, and tried to snatch the knife away. "Give that back! How dare you use my dagger without asking!"

Balsa grabbed his hand in hers, and with a flick of her wrist, sent him flying into the grass. He groaned and tried to rise, but she bent over him, pinning him down, her right hand on his neck and her knee on his chest. She held his gaze steadily. "It's about time you stopped running away." He clenched his teeth and inhaled shakily, his eyes brimming with tears. "You feel like crying, don't you?" she said quietly. "Your heart is so heavy you can hardly bear it. You feel utterly helpless, yet at the same time, you're filled with a rage that seems beyond your control. Am I right? But taking your anger out on others is not going to make you feel any better, because you aren't that stupid. If you keep on like this, the uselessness of it will just build up inside you, making it even worse. So stop running and take a good look at yourself. Look at what is making you so angry."

Chagum closed his eyes. Tears trickled slowly down his cheeks toward his ears. Hiccupping, he whispered, "Damn everything!"

Balsa let him go and stood up. He lay there, his arms crossed over his face. She returned to the rabbit and, when she had finished skinning it, washed the knife and began sharpening it. Chagum came up and stood behind her, staring absently at her hands. She spoke quietly, keeping her eyes on the knife. "If you sharpen a blade, it cuts better. This is a fact. If only all things in life were so logical."

She turned the blade to the sun, and it flashed as the light caught the metal. "Sometimes a kind person who lived a good and peaceful life is killed by some good-for-nothing who spent his entire life sponging off his family. You won't find any fairness in this world." Chagum crouched down beside her. "When I was young, I used to get mad too, and take it out on Jiguro. Why did my father have to be killed? Why was I forced to keep moving from one place to the next, cold and hungry, when I hadn't done anything to deserve it? Thinking about that always made me angry. But after a few years, I couldn't even take my anger out on Jiguro anymore, because I realized he was even less fortunate than I was. All these terrible hardships had been forced on him just because he was my father's friend. When I saw that, I thought there was no hope for me at all. Now my guilt for making Jiguro suffer was added to everything else."

Chagum felt a pang in the pit of his stomach. Balsa had been paid to protect him; that was all. Yet he had behaved like a spoiled brat, venting his rage at her without a second thought, and she had let him, though she was not even his mother. Shame coursed through him, as cold as snow.

But Balsa turned toward him and smiled. "When I was sixteen, I told Jiguro that we should split up. I was old enough, I said, to protect myself. If my enemies should find and defeat me, then it was my fate to die. Jiguro had done enough. Let's go back to being strangers, I told him. Live for yourself, I said."

"And what did he say?" Chagum whispered.

"He told me that it was about time I stopped trying to keep accounts, weighing so much misfortune against so much happiness, or thinking about how in debt I was to him for something he had done. He said it was meaningless to try to settle accounts for days gone by, as if you were counting money. 'I'm here,' he said, 'because I don't actually mind living with you like this. That's all. You see.'"

She wiped the dagger on a cloth and handed it to Chagum. "And now look at me. Despite his advice, I've been incredibly stupid. I've wasted a lot of time calculating the value of human life in the cash I'm paid as a bodyguard. No matter how many lives I saved, how could I ever feel free?" She put her hand on his shoulder. "But you know, right now I feel much better. Being your bodyguard has helped me understand for the first time how Jiguro felt."

The weight of Balsa's hand on his shoulder felt good. With a sigh of relief, Chagum slipped the dagger into his belt and breathed in deeply. He felt his lungs fill with the fresh and bracing fragrance of budding leaves.

Two months passed. The snow on the mountains disappeared; the trees turned a deeper green with each passing day, and the breeze blew gentle and fragrant. Balsa had braced herself for further changes in Chagum, but nothing seemed to happen. When Torogai reappeared, smelling of dusty earth, the egg was still the same. After listening to them recount their winter, Torogai snorted. "Of course it didn't keep on changing! Do you think he could stand it if it did? Just you wait and see — I bet there's another major change in a month or so. But you know what?" she said to him. "You don't seem much like a prince anymore. In fact, you look just like an ordinary kid."

Chagum glared at her, but then suddenly he noticed that her head was far lower than his. "Wait a minute!" he exclaimed. "Did you shrink?"

"Are you kidding? I'm not getting any smaller than this. You've grown, you idiot!"

Balsa looked at Chagum in surprise. "She's right. You've grown a lot."

"The new year has already passed, so you must be, what, twelve, Chagum?" Tanda asked. "That's the stage when boys change the most."

His words reminded Balsa of a day long ago. She had always looked on the little boy Tanda as her younger brother, but just after he turned twelve, he shot up suddenly, overtaking her height before she knew it. She remembered staring at him in surprise when he spoke with a man's deep voice, knowing that something decisive had changed.

Not long after Torogai reappeared, she dragged Tanda off on another trip to meet the Juchi Ro Gai. But once again their journey was in vain. Even the creatures that lived in the mud of Nayugu seemed to fear Rarunga, for they would not speak of it at all. By the time they returned through Yashiro village, spring had passed, and the humming of the cicadas echoed through the fields and mountains, heralding the arrival of summer.

As they stepped out of the forest onto the riverbank, Tanda stopped, shocked by the sight that lay before them. By now, the fields, which had been planted months before, should have been filled with a waving sea of tender, green rice stalks. Instead, there was nothing but bare, cracked earth, which had turned a chalky brown. Only the small fields closest to the river were still filled with water, and these grew only a meager amount of rice. It was certainly not enough to feed the entire village.

"Look at that," Tanda murmured.

Torogai gazed grimly at the fields. "If this continues, many will die when fall comes."

A man was walking down from the terraced fields that

spread up the steep slope. He waved when he caught sight of them and quickened his pace. It was Yuga, whose daughter Nina had told Tanda the story of Nyunga Ro Im.

"Torogai! Tanda! It's been a long time." He bowed his head in greeting and then glanced at the fields. His stubble-covered face darkened, and in his tightly pursed lips they could see the anxiety of someone keenly aware of impending disaster and yet helpless to avert it. "Terrible, isn't it? It's the same everywhere, they say. It hasn't rained as much as a bug's pee since spring. Just the sun beating down every day." He hastily apologized to the sun god for complaining, then stood staring at the fields for a while, as if he had forgotten they were there.

Finally his gaze returned to Tanda. "This is what you meant when you were talking with Nina, wasn't it? About the Nayugu cloud spirit inside my great-uncle. That story was true then, wasn't it?"

Tanda nodded. Yuga grimaced. "Damnation!" he exclaimed. "I've never seen a drought like this before, never! Even the elders have never seen anything like it. There's a saying that the crops will grow as long as there's sunshine, but there's no hope for the rice crop this year. If the weather stays like this, we'll even lose the rice in those fields over there.

"In the new year, word came from the Star Palace that we should prepare for a drought, so we quickly planted *shiga* and *yassha*. Even so, we'll barely have enough. There's no way we can buy rice or barley from the merchants, especially with the prices gone through the roof. Some merchants are even refusing to sell what they've kept stored away, since you can't eat money."

He sighed and looked at them. His eyes were bloodshot. "I don't suppose you could make it rain for us with your magic weaving?" Tears welled in his eyes. "If this goes on any longer, my baby son won't make it through the fall!"

Torogai looked at him, but all she could say was, "We're doing the best we can."

CHAPTER IV
ON THE TRAIL OF *SHIGU SALUA*

Summer was beginning by the time Shuga found the tale of Nyunga Ro Im engraved on the stone tablets of Nanai's memoirs. As he read it aloud, tracing the letters in the stone with his finger, he could not keep his hand from shaking. This was it! The water spirit mentioned in the legend of the sacred ancestor and the founding of the country; the thing that the Yakoo magic weaver had referred to as "the egg." This at last would give him the answers he sought.

But as he painstakingly read the story, stumbling over unfamiliar words, he discovered that the facts were very different from the legend he knew. When the "portent of dryness" that foretold a great drought appeared in the sky, Nanai himself had gone into the mountains to find the Yakoo, leaving the construction of the capital in the hands of a trusted few. There he met a young boy who bore an egg in his breast and a group of Yakoo who were guarding him. Just once every hundred years, the Yakoo told Nanai, humans were given the chance to aid the workings of the universe. This was a great blessing, they said. They taught him about the worlds of Sagu and Nayugu and how the egg of Nyunga Ro Im begins to grow when winter ends, causing changes in its host. Around the same time, the Egg Eater, Rarunga of Nayugu, starts to move, like a snake hunting birds' eggs. Everything Shuga read confirmed the truth of the Yakoo story.

As he realized what a terrible mistake he and the Master Star Reader had made, he broke into a cold sweat. *What month is it?* he thought suddenly. He raised his eyes from the stone tablet and gazed up at the dark ceiling. When did he last eat? He had to remember! What had it been like outside? *It's already the month of the cicada's song! There are less than twenty days left until midsummer. Is Rarunga already hunting the prince?* It took him at least half a day to decipher a single stone tablet, sometimes a whole day. At this rate, it would take him ten more days to find out how Nanai and the Yakoo managed to destroy the Egg Eater and save the egg!

Calm down, he chided himself. *The Master Star Reader has already sent the Hunters after the prince. Right now, the most important thing is to learn every fact I can.*

And thus he immersed himself in deciphering the tablets, sparing no time for either food or sleep. Two days later he stumbled upon a crucial fact and raised his eyes from the tablet. Although his head ached as if it might break in two, he paused in thought and then climbed unsteadily up the ladder to the room above. The Master Star Reader was just returning to his room to sleep. He started back in surprise when he saw Shuga emerge from the trapdoor. "Shuga! What's wrong? You look so pale!"

Shuga staggered and sank to the floor. Supporting him, the Master Star Reader bent his ear to his mouth to catch what he was saying. A light kindled in his eyes and he nodded eagerly. "Yes, of course. You did well, Shuga. I'll send a message to the Hunters so they can get there first. This time it will all work out," he reassured him, patting him gently on the back. "Reading the tablets is very important, but first you must rest. If you collapse, there will be no one left to uncover their secrets."

Shuga raised his bloodshot eyes and pleaded, "Master Star Reader, we're racing against time. Couldn't you read them for me?"

The Master Star Reader thought for a moment but then shook his head. "Like you, I have no time. I've been so busy trying to save the life of the First Prince that I haven't had any rest either. Tonight is the first time I've been permitted to sleep, and I must be by his side again tomorrow."

Shuga nodded, so tired he felt faint. He could do no more.

"You can sleep here tonight. I'll have some bedding put out for you. Go straight to bed. There's no need to wait up for me."

Although Shuga vaguely remembered him leaving the room, he immediately collapsed into a deep sleep.

The next change in Chagum occurred one hot, sticky morning five days after Torogai and Tanda returned from their trip.

This time when he complained of being tired, no one was deeply concerned — not even Chagum himself. It was as if a long-awaited day had finally arrived. He slept for only a few hours, and woke to find himself filled with a strange compulsion. "Something's calling me," he said. "It's a bit like that feeling I used to have, the feeling of wanting to go home. I just know I have to go — as if I'm being called there."

"Who's calling you?" Balsa asked, but Chagum shook his head, perplexed.

"It's hard to describe, but it doesn't feel like a person. It's more like being pulled by an invisible thread. And I feel like I've got to follow it."

"Sounds just like the *toburya* in the Aoyumi River," said Torogai. "The young fish swim out to sea, then climb back up the river again to lay their eggs. Nyunga Ro Im's egg is being drawn toward what it needs in the same way. The knowledge must have been planted inside it from the very beginning, the same way birds know the route they must travel. Chagum, which way do you want to go?"

Without any hesitation, he pointed. Torogai frowned. "That's odd. I thought it would be toward the sea, but it seems I was wrong. I guess there must be something you have to do before the egg goes there. Well, we have no choice but to do what it wants."

They hurriedly cleaned up the cave and prepared to travel. Looking around the big empty room, barren now even of the ashes swept from the hearth, Chagum felt a cold loneliness. He looked up at Balsa, who had hoisted her bag onto her back. "Balsa?"

"What?"

"If the egg hatches safely and I'm no longer needed, do you think we could come back here again? Can I live with you and Tanda?"

Balsa was glad Tanda had gone outside. "Well, that's certainly one possibility," she answered noncommittally and pushed him gently toward the door. "Come on. It's time to go."

"All right."

Chagum had grown so much sturdier since she had met him last autumn that there was really no comparison. He could now light a fire by himself, and thanks to their

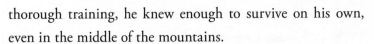

thorough training, he knew enough to survive on his own, even in the middle of the mountains.

As he followed the others along the mountain path, Chagum occasionally glimpsed strange sights. When he focused his attention on them, he could see Nayugu spreading out before him, superimposed on the solid world of Sagu. That other world was much more rugged than Sagu. Mountains towered black against the sky, mist climbing slowly toward their peaks. There were no roads that could be traversed by humans, and the land was devoid of any sign of people. As he walked along a cliff path looking down into a valley in Sagu, he saw it superimposed over a valley in Nayugu — one so deep and dark it appeared bottomless. Occasionally he sensed something squirming in the damp obscurity that concealed the valley floor. But what he saw of Nayugu was not always frightening. At times, its beauty moved him profoundly. Its water was as blue as lapis lazuli and so deep it seemed to go on forever. Its flowers bloomed in vivid colors, as if proud to be alive. The air was so clear and sweet it refreshed his spirit.

"Hey! Chagum! Watch where you're going!" Balsa grabbed his arm and he started in surprise. Trying to avoid a large rock in Nayugu, he had almost stepped right off the cliff. He hastily stopped looking at the other world.

That night as they sat around the fire, with green grass spread on top to smoke out the mosquitoes, Chagum related what he had seen. "You're so lucky!" Tanda exclaimed. "What a fantastic opportunity. Not even the greatest magic weavers can see Nayugu so easily. I wish I could see it like you."

"No kidding!" Torogai chimed in. "It's totally wasted on a kid like him!"

"Chagum," Balsa interrupted. "When you're looking at Nayugu, can you see any sign of Rarunga, the Egg Eater?"

"No, none at all."

Balsa looked at Tanda. "It's almost midsummer, and Chagum has started to move. I expected Rarunga to appear almost immediately, but I don't feel anything. Do you?"

"No. It's almost worse than if we did."

Torogai snorted. "Ha! Don't be ridiculous. It's going to turn up sooner or later even if you beg it not to. Just keep your eyes peeled. That goes for the kid too."

She was right, but just because they saw no sign of the monster did not mean they could rest easy. Tanda and Balsa decided to take turns sleeping.

They continued walking west through the Misty Blue Mountains. On the fourth day, they came to the upper reaches of the Aoyumi River.

"The water is so low," Balsa murmured. Judging by the watermarks on the boulders, it was only a third of its normal depth, and the exposed rocks, bleached white by the relentless sun, made her uneasy. As they walked on, they discussed the drought, but Chagum paid little heed to their voices. As soon as he saw the clear stream running through the damp, mossy stones, he had felt his heart begin to throb. The rushing water sent up a white spray where it crashed against the boulders, and the smell of water enveloped him. *It's this way. There's no mistake. We're almost there.* For some reason, he felt his mouth fill with saliva.

Tanda turned to Balsa and said, "We should reach Aoike Pond around noon. The *shigu salua* will be blooming there at this time of year."

"*Shigu salua?*" Balsa murmured. Something stirred in her memory.

Chagum's pace quickened. The other three glanced at each other. He seemed to be headed for that very pond and broke into a run when they caught their first glimpse of it through the trees. Ordinarily, they would have stopped him; running made it harder to detect an enemy. But they had seen no signs that they were being followed, and they were so distracted by Chagum and their curiosity about what he would do that even Torogai neglected caution.

A grassy glade surrounded the large pond, and just as Tanda had predicted, the water near the banks was covered in small white *shigu salua* flowers, floating on their round green leaves. They gave off a peculiar and overpowering smell — the heavy scent of water, like the wind after a summer downpour. Instantly, Balsa remembered: It was this scent that had clung to Chagum when she had stopped him from stumbling out Toya's door — the scent of *shigu salua*.

The scene that Chagum saw at that moment was very different from the one his companions saw. Before him in Nayugu lay a body of water as big as a lake, with a surface like a deep blue mirror. Superimposed on this he could still see the pond in Sagu. Faint ripples disturbed its surface whenever a breeze passed over the lake in Nayugu.

Chagum rushed over to the flowers and inhaled deeply. Their fragrance was intoxicating. From among the many blossoms floating on the pond, he found the one that bloomed in both worlds, the one that spanned Nayugu and Sagu simultaneously. Plucking it, he shoved it into his mouth and devoured it with rapture. The nectar was far more abundant than he had expected from the size of the flower. As it trickled down his throat, an odd warmth spread slowly through him, and he sat down abruptly on the bank, as if he were drunk.

The others watched him wordlessly from start to finish. Suddenly Balsa gripped the spear in her hand tightly. She knew intuitively that they were surrounded.

"Balsa, don't do it," Torogai whispered. "I know. We've been trapped. But you mustn't try to cut your way through with your spear."

"Why?" Balsa asked sharply, her eyes still fixed on Chagum so their enemies would not realize they had been discovered.

"This trap was set before we even got here. That can only mean one thing. The Star Readers have found some record of how they destroyed Rarunga two hundred years ago. I want to know how they did it."

"But I can feel their hostility. They may not mean to harm Chagum, but they most certainly intend to kill us."

"I know. So we'll just have to make Chagum our hostage."

Balsa looked at Tanda. Although slightly tense, he looked ready to meet whatever might come their way.

"There are eight of them," he said. "Torogai has already tricked them once, and I doubt they'll fall for that again. I guess we have no choice but to do as she suggests."

Balsa nodded finally and then bent toward Chagum. "Can you hear me, Chagum?" He looked up at her, his eyes glazed. "The Mikado's men have found us. It looks like they don't mean to kill you, but they do plan to kill the rest of us." Apprehension finally registered in his eyes. "So we're going to make you our hostage. Will you trust us?"

Chagum pressed his lips together tightly and nodded. Still drunk on the nectar, he stared blankly at the trees and saw several figures appear. Four Hunters surrounded them, their short bows held at the ready. Although they had a limited range, the quick bows could be fired in rapid succession, which made them an ideal weapon in a forest such as this, where there was not much space.

The other four Hunters moved toward them slowly.

Jin held a blowgun; his wounds had already healed. Yun carried a long sword in one hand and a dagger in the other. The scar Balsa's spear had scored across his face was still livid, and he glared at her, making no attempt to conceal the hatred that seethed inside him. Zen was empty-handed, but she could see by the way his knees were braced that he would not be caught off guard. They knew her ability only too well now; there was not a trace of overconfidence in their stance.

At Mon's signal, Jin, Zen, and Yun began to close in. They walked so as not to obstruct the archers' line of fire, and it was obvious that they knew every inch of ground, the location of every rock. While Balsa had no intention of disobeying Torogai's warning not to wield her spear, she still probed carefully for some way to break through their line. But the magic weaver was right; it was impossible. Although she might have stood a chance on her own, as a group they had no possibility of winning against eight men like these.

Torogai waited until the Hunters were about to pounce before she yelled. "Stop right there!"

The very air seemed to freeze. The Hunters, still poised to strike, halted in their tracks.

"Magic weaver, your tricks won't work anymore," Mon said in a strong, clear voice.

Torogai grinned. "I'm not so foolish as to use the same trick twice." She looked so perfectly at ease, it made the Hunters uncomfortable. "Listen carefully! We have no intention of fighting. To be honest, we have no time for that right now. We must meet with the Master Star Reader as soon as possible."

Mon had not foreseen this turn of events, but he was too smart to let it show. "Enough of your nonsense!" he barked. "We're the ones in charge here, not you."

"Fine then. Get on with it! But I should warn you that the instant one of us is either injured or killed, the prince's heart will stop beating, regardless of whether he sees it happen or not. As long as you understand that, we'll do whatever you say."

"There's no use bluffing," Mon retorted.

Torogai grinned wickedly — a smile so gruesome it made them shudder. "If you don't believe me, why don't you check it out as we talk? Go ahead. Try it and see what kind of magic old Torogai has woven around the prince."

Mon realized they were at a disadvantage; these three knew the prince's value. "You think you've won, magic weaver," he said quietly. "Feel free to think that. Our job is to return the prince to the Master Star Reader. You've said that you'll come quietly, so come. You'll save us a lot of trouble. But remember: The Star Palace is a sacred place, where your dirty magic tricks are worthless."

He signaled the other Hunters to surround the captives, leaving no room for escape. They began walking. Balsa gripped her spear in her right hand, while with her left arm she supported Chagum, who was still unsteady on his feet. The Hunters, who had come expecting to take revenge on her, ground their teeth in frustration, but they were not so foolish as to let their feelings show.

Everyone, including Balsa, was sure that they would arrive at the Star Palace without incident.

CHAPTER V
ATTACKING CLAWS

They continued walking, Jin in front, Yun and Zen on either side, and Mon behind them. The four other Hunters were nowhere to be seen. Balsa knew they were probably shadowing them through the forest on all four sides, an extremely difficult feat in this rugged terrain. The cicadas' chorus beat down upon them, a constant buzzing in their ears.

Chagum was still in a daze. Although he was aware that he was moving along the mountain path with Balsa's hand gripping his arm, at times the scenery of Sagu vanished so completely that all he could see was Nayugu. His body reeked so strongly of *shigu salua* it was almost nauseating, but the scent could only be detected in Nayugu; not even Balsa, who was right beside him, was aware of it. It lingered on the ground with every step he took, leaving a clear trail behind him.

Suddenly Balsa felt her flesh crawl, the hair rising on the nape of her neck as if she'd been doused in cold water. She braced herself, thinking at first that Mon was about to attack her, but she immediately knew she was wrong: Everyone had come to a stop. While the Hunters, Torogai, and Tanda clearly sensed something as well — a presence that seemed to seep like vapor from the ground — none of them could pinpoint its source. The thunderous racket of the cicadas hushed instantly, and the sudden silence was unbearably shrill.

Chagum's heart constricted with terror. Something in Nayugu was watching him. He knew he should look into that other world with a steady gaze, but his fear was so great that he shut it out instinctively.

"Ba-Balsa!" He cowered, clinging to her. She pointed her spear at the ground. Malice seethed beneath her, not from just one place, but many! Yet she could see nothing. Something gleamed at Chagum's feet — *there!* — and Balsa stabbed it with her spear. The point struck something hard, but whatever it was vanished instantly. Her spear stuck in the ground, and she had to stop to pull it out again.

Suddenly, claws as tall as a man appeared around them. Slicing through vines, shrubs, even tree roots, they rushed straight for Chagum. At once, Balsa grabbed him by his belt and threw him up into the air. One of the claws barely

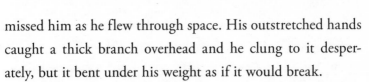

missed him as he flew through space. His outstretched hands caught a thick branch overhead and he clung to it desperately, but it bent under his weight as if it would break.

Balsa's speed astounded the Hunters. One moment she drove her spear into the ground, and the next she vaulted into the air. Stepping on the spear's hilt, she leapt onto a limb above Chagum's head, then reached down and grabbed him by the collar, hauling him up into the top of the tree. Beneath them the claws closed in on all sides, clumps of earth flying through the air toward the trunk.

Then they suddenly disappeared. They did not sink back into the earth, but simply vanished, leaving an ominous emptiness behind. Yun lay screaming and writhing on the ground, his right leg ripped open. His sword had shattered from its impact with the claws.

Tanda and Torogai chanted under their breath. When they opened their eyes to Nayugu, they saw a soft, muddy swamp that stretched as far as they could see. A creature resembling a giant spider scuttled toward them on six legs. On its back, a ring of six claws surrounded a mouth from which thin tentacles waved like whips, making a hissing sound. This was Rarunga, and it was far more horrible than either of the magic weavers had imagined. Returning their consciousness to Sagu, they shouted, "Get up into the trees! Hurry!"

But Jin stood rooted to the ground, uncomprehending, his sword still held at the ready. As Tanda ran toward him,

the claws suddenly reappeared. Just before one of them could slice Jin in two, Tanda shoved him out of the way.

Blood spurted from Tanda's side. Balsa's face paled as she watched. "Chagum, hold on tight to this branch and *don't move*, all right?" She leapt to the ground and ran over to Tanda. Sticking her arms under his, she hauled him up to a standing position. He groaned and looked back at her.

"I'm all right! I'm all right! Leave me alone! You should be guarding Chagum!" He tried to push her away, but she ignored him. From her perch in the tree, she had watched Rarunga's movements and seen that its claws always appeared in a circle with Chagum at its center. Guessing that it would not bother to pursue anyone besides Chagum, she hoisted Tanda over her shoulder and ran.

But in those few minutes, a third and drastic change had come over Chagum. Nurtured by the nectar of the *shigu salua*, the egg was almost ready to hatch. For Chagum, this transformation was far quicker and more terrifying than anything before. He noticed with surprise that all sensation was receding from his hands and feet; soon he could no longer feel the bark where his hands gripped the tree. He tried to scream, but no noise came out. The sounds around him grew distant and his vision darkened; the five senses that linked him to the outer world faded away until he lost touch with them completely. His consciousness shrank into an endless expanse of darkness, and in its place, some other will began to move his hands, his feet, his body. At first, he was so terrified he thought he would go insane, but gradually he even lost the sensation of fear, until his mind fell into a state closely resembling sleep.

Still he struggled to keep his own consciousness as though fighting off drowsiness. His efforts were rewarded, for he seemed to reach some form of understanding with this other will. Although his perception was disjointed, he glimpsed snatches of what was happening around him, like someone bobbing to the surface from deep underwater. He saw the ground below him sway as it flashed out of sight behind him. He glimpsed his right hand grasping a vine-covered branch, then it vanished and the river rushed up at him, the rocks jutting out of the low water. Water sprayed into the air. In response to its smell, hot power rose from the depths of his being, and Chagum's mind entered a strange world in which he was destined to wander for some time.

Balsa laid Tanda down where she thought he would be safe. When she finally looked back, she saw Chagum receding rapidly into the distance as he swung through the trees like a monkey, flying from branch to branch with incredible agility. For a brief moment, she stood there stunned. His movements were not human; even she could never have swung so lightly through the forest. And he was hurtling away . . .

She pulled herself back to her senses and raced off in the direction in which he had disappeared. Without warning, a huge claw towered above her, blocking her way and raining

clods of earth down upon her. Holding her hand before her
face to protect her eyes from the dirt, she nimbly dodged to
one side and ran past it. Behind her, she heard the Hunters'
screams. Even such seasoned warriors stood little chance
against a monster that could vanish at will, and Rarunga
seemed to have recognized that it must kill them all before it
could eat.

Balsa followed doggedly after Chagum, but as she had to
watch out for claws that attacked unexpectedly and tentacles
that tried to entangle her, the distance between them rapidly
widened. She clenched her teeth and kept running. Suddenly
she noticed that dirt no longer flew through the air. She
seemed to have escaped beyond the circle of the claws. Behind
her, the monster was still thrashing about wildly. *Rarunga
doesn't know Chagum has escaped*, she suddenly realized.
Maybe it can't follow someone who has left the ground. She
peered through the gaps between the trees, searching for
Chagum, but he was nowhere to be seen. She calmed her
breathing and probed for him using all her senses. Far in the
distance, she thought she heard something splash into water.
Of course! He must have been running toward the river!

She raced through the trees until she burst out onto its
banks. There she stopped in surprise. A veil of mist, as thick
as smoke, rose above the river, hiding everything under a
white fog all the way upstream. It obscured her view so completely that she could see nothing at all, let alone Chagum.

"Chagum!" She shouted his name until she was hoarse, but the mist absorbed the sound and no answer came.

She had only taken her eyes off him for a minute. That was all. How could she have known it would have such consequences as this? She stood motionless, stricken with remorse.

CHAPTER VI
NANAI'S MEMOIRS REVISITED

Mon gazed wordlessly at the awful sight before him. Yun's leg was badly gored. The other Hunters had been scattered in all directions. Two were seriously wounded by the claws, while another two had suffered more minor injuries. By the time Rarunga had vanished for good, only Mon, Jin, and Zen were left unscathed.

Torogai took out a bottle of strong spirits to use as a disinfectant, sterilized a needle and thread, and deftly sewed up the gash in Tanda's side. Then she turned her attention to the other wounded men. Fighting the searing pain, Tanda rose to help her.

"I don't see Balsa or Chagum, Tanda. You'd better go look for them," Torogai urged him, but he shook his head.

"I'll look, but not until we're done with these two.

They'll die if they aren't treated now. Balsa will get along without me for a while longer."

Torogai did not press him any further. Jin, Zen, and Mon split up, each helping one of their injured comrades. When they had done all they could for the time being, Tanda heard someone stalking toward them through the forest. He stood up hastily and saw that it was Balsa. Looking very grim, she strode quickly over to her spear and yanked it from the ground.

"Balsa! What happened to Chagum?" Tanda asked. "Isn't he with you?" She gave him a sharp glance and shook her head shortly. "What happened?"

She walked over to him, frowning, and then sighed. "I don't know. He just ran away." She told him everything from start to finish. Torogai and the Hunters drew near to listen.

"He must have manipulated the water," Torogai said. "You told me he did that before, remember?"

"Yes. But it only happened when he was asleep or unconscious."

Torogai's eyes narrowed. "Then perhaps he's not conscious."

"What?"

"In the beginning, the egg of Nyunga Ro Im only took over Chagum's body when he was asleep or unconscious, right? But when the second change took place, Chagum felt the egg's impulses as his own actions, even when he was awake, and he could see Nayugu with ease."

"So you think that another change has taken place," Tanda said.

Torogai nodded. "There is just one day left until mid-summer — one day until the egg hatches. The egg has probably taken over his body and is controlling his actions to make sure it's safely born."

Balsa slammed the butt of her spear on the ground. Everyone jumped and looked at her in surprise. "Who the *hell* does this Nyunga Ro Im think it is?" she shouted. "I don't give a damn about the cloud spirit! If anything happens to Chagum, I'll smash that egg before Rarunga can eat it! How dare it mess with someone else's life like this!"

Torogai glanced at Tanda as if to say that it was his job to make this crazy spear-wielder calm down. She did not wait to see him shrug, but instead turned to look sharply at the leader of the Hunters. Mon returned her gaze boldly.

"You there!" Torogai said. "You saw those claws. I don't know what orders the Master Star Reader gave you, but that's the monster Mikado Torugaru supposedly killed off long ago. It's after the cloud spirit's egg, which is inside the prince." Briefly, she explained what had happened so far and the worlds of Sagu and Nayugu. The Hunters listened intently without uttering a word. It was an astonishing tale, one that dispelled all their doubts. "And that," she concluded, "is why I must see the Master Star Reader and find out how they defeated it. But I'm worried about the prince. Balsa and Tanda are a hard pair to beat, but the more fighters they have, the better. Would any of you be willing to help them find the prince?"

"As if you needed to ask," Mon growled. "I'll go with them myself."

But Jin stepped forward. "Let me do it, sir."

"And me, sir," Zen added quietly.

Mon nodded. If there were two, at least one of them could always contact him, and his first duty was to report immediately to the Mikado and the Master Star Reader and let them know what had transpired. Once that decision was made, everything fell rapidly into place. "We'll leave the badly wounded here," Mon said. "Taga, Sune, you stay with them through the night. I'll take the magic weaver to the capital. As soon as we reach it, I'll send help. If her story is true, that thing with the claws is after the prince, so it shouldn't attack those of you who stay here. All right?"

The Hunters nodded. Jin and Zen set off silently with Balsa and Tanda while Mon and Torogai started off at a run toward the capital. Theirs was an amazing journey. They were more than thirty miles from the capital at Kosenkyo, separated from it by rugged mountains that would normally take even the Hunters half a day to travel; but they raced through the crags as if they were running across a flat plain. While Torogai was amazingly strong for someone over seventy, she could not run all the way without resting, and when evening approached and she began to tire, Mon carried her on his back.

Mon could not stop thinking about the First Prince, who was still critically ill. It was all very well to talk about this Nyunga-whatever and its egg, but if anything should happen to the First Prince, then Chagum would be the Mikado's sole remaining heir. He must be protected at all costs. As he sped along the mountain path in the pitch dark, Mon suddenly wondered if his own ancestors had once run through the mountains like this, hunting the same beast two hundred years ago.

It was almost dawn when they finally reached the capital. Torogai, who had slept most of the way on his back, felt greatly revived, but Mon was so exhausted he thought he would collapse. They were guided to the secret room under the Mikado's chambers, but the Master Star Reader was unable to meet them: The First Prince had taken a turn for the worse, and he could not leave his side. Torogai had just cursed him roundly when a young Star Reader entered the room.

It was Shuga. Mon was startled by his appearance; he looked like an invalid who was wasting away, his face pallid and his cheeks sunken. Still, he listened attentively to what Mon told him, nodding at the end of his report. "Thank goodness you made it in time," he said. "Sending you on ahead to Aoike Pond was the right decision. You did well,

Mon. I'll send word as soon as the Master Star Reader returns. In the meantime, you should get some rest."

Mon hesitated for a moment, wondering if it was all right to leave this young Star Reader alone with the magic weaver — he looked so drawn and frail. But the Master Star Reader obviously trusted him to act in his place, and the firm set of his jaw and shrewd expression convinced Mon that he could handle Torogai. He bowed. "Thank you," he said. "I appreciate the opportunity to rest."

When Mon had left the room, Shuga turned to the old magic weaver and said, "You must be Torogai. I've wanted to meet you for a long time."

She snorted derisively. "What about Rarunga?" she demanded. "Did you find out how to destroy it?"

Shuga shook his head, his face grave.

"What?" Torogai exclaimed. "Don't tell me you don't know!"

A flicker of anger passed across Shuga's face, but it vanished quickly into an expression of deep anxiety and fatigue. "No, I don't know. Or rather, I could not find out — because Nanai and Torugaru didn't destroy Rarunga."

Torogai's mouth dropped open in surprise. "They didn't destroy it? Then how could the egg have hatched safely?"

"Magic weaver of the Yakoo, Nanai's memoirs are written in ancient Yogoese. There are parts I cannot completely comprehend. I was able to decipher up to where the egg was born, and I also gathered that Rarunga is a kind of creature that lives in the mud of a land called Nayugu. But there are too many letters and words that I don't understand."

Torogai leaned forward eagerly. "Perhaps it uses a lot of Yakoo names for things. Tell me that part and maybe I can help you."

Shuga nodded, and they settled on the floor. Torogai thought that Shuga would have to go and get the memoirs, but to her surprise, the Star Reader closed his eyes and began to recite from memory.

"*Siguru — the Yakoo child who bore the egg of Nyunga Ro Im — went to Aoike Pond and ate the* shigu salua. *As the magic weavers and I made to follow in the child's footsteps, we were attacked by Rarunga. . . .*" Shuga spoke smoothly, flawlessly interpreting the ancient Yogoese into modern vernacular while preserving the rhythm of the old language. Torogai felt her skin crawl as she realized that what had happened to them yesterday was exactly what had happened two centuries ago.

"*Siguru escaped into a tree and thus was he saved. The magic weavers wove their charms to see the world of Nayugu. 'This is an ill-fated spot,' they cried, and carrying Siguru on their backs, they escaped from that land. Rarunga, they said, could smell the egg and track the scent from Siguru's feet, which penetrated the land of Nayugu; wherefore they bore him on their backs.*"

Torogai slapped her knee and exclaimed, "Of course, the

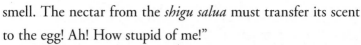

smell. The nectar from the *shigu salua* must transfer its scent to the egg! Ah! How stupid of me!"

Shuga continued, ignoring her outburst. *"Siguru reached the land of Sahnan as midsummer drew nigh. Oh, beautiful Sahnan with its bubbling blue spring, source of the Aoyumi River! A small spring it was, but in this summer when drought gripped all the land, its pure water was the single thread of life for all living things. There a thousand birds, a thousand creatures slaked their thirst . . .*

"But in the land of Nayugu, Sahnan was a great muddy swamp spreading endlessly in all directions. This, this was the very home of Rarunga. Brave Siguru! Boldly did he set foot on Sahnan.

"Now was the time to do as had been done since ancient times — to bear four bright torches and surround Sahnan, keeping Rarunga at bay. But woe betide us, for the power of Nyunga Ro Im that lay inside Siguru created a white mist over the water's source, and try though we might to light the torches, it was to no avail.

"Ah, woe! We could do naught but bewail our helplessness as Rarunga's claws rent Siguru asunder. . . ."

Torugai's head jerked up suddenly. "What?! You mean he died? You're telling me that he was *killed*?!"

Shuga nodded, his face grim. "Yes, the boy died. I expect that this is why, in our legend, the blood of the boy possessed by the demon runs into the water's source."

Torogai gnashed her teeth. "Damn! How could this be true? When I asked the Water Dwellers of Nayugu about it many, many years ago, they told me the egg hatched and the Yakoo boy didn't die."

"Is that so? And did they tell you how Rarunga was destroyed?"

"They didn't know! Besides, it's impossible to talk with them for very long because it's so hard to stay between Sagu and Nayugu."

Shuga shook his head slowly. "Then perhaps some children in the past did survive. But the boy two hundred years ago died."

"Well then, what about the egg? Was it eaten?"

Shuga groaned. "No. That's just it. It wasn't. Magic weaver, do you know of a creature called *nahjiru*? In fact, I don't even know if it's a creature. It may be another name for the wind."

"*Nahjiru? Nahjiru.* No, I've never heard of it."

Shuga frowned. "You don't know? Of all people, I thought that you at least would be able to tell me. If I knew what it was, I would understand a little better what happened."

"Well, I'm sorry! You're not the only one who's disappointed, you know. But tell me what that part says, the part with the *nahjiru* in it."

Shuga nodded and, closing his eyes once again, began reciting from the memoirs.

"The Yakoo magic weaver, heeding not his own safety, leapt inside Rarunga's claws, snatched the egg from the torn body of Siguru, and threw it up, up into the heavens. Then came the nahjiru, *and seizing the egg, it sped south far across the sky. Ah, this, in truth, is the law of the universe. The egg carried by* nahjiru *is returned to the deep, deep sea to breathe clouds into the heavens. . . .*

"Ah, this, in truth, is the law of the universe. Soft clouds billow in the heavens of Sagu, sweet rain falls to revive the earth."

Torogai, who had been lost in thought, suddenly exclaimed, "That's it! Of course! Now I understand. That's what it's all about. Damn!" She groaned. Shuga leaned forward eagerly.

"You understand? What is this *nahjiru*? Tell me."

Torogai raised her face and hit the floor with her fist. "What a fool I've been! How can I call myself a magic weaver when I didn't even notice something like this?" She fixed Shuga with a piercing stare and told him what *nahjiru* meant, and how they could defeat Rarunga according to the passage he had just recited.

When she had finished, Shuga's face was even paler. How could he have missed this vital point when he had spent so much time studying Nanai's memoirs? It was ironic: Torogai had read too much into the Star Readers' schemes, while Shuga had totally dismissed the Yakoo lore. As a result, they had both overlooked the wisdom concealed within something the two cultures shared: the ancient midsummer festival.

"I've failed," Shuga said. "It's too far to reach Sahnan now. Even if this method succeeds, we have no way of telling them in time."

Torogai stood up. "There is one way, though I don't know whether it will work or not. Still, it's worth a try."

"What is it?"

"I can ask the Water Dwellers of Nayugu to take them a message. I'm sure my apprentice will understand it." She turned abruptly to look at Shuga's puzzled, anxious face. "I doubt I'll have another chance to speak like this with a Star Reader, so I'm going to be frank while I have the chance. This time, don't try to hide the truth just for the sake of your stupid politics. I can't stand the thought of putting people through this same ordeal a hundred years from now."

Shuga averted his eyes for a second, then met her gaze squarely. "I'll do my best. Let me promise you this, Yakoo magic weaver: When I become Master Star Reader someday, I will find a way to make sure the truth is passed down." Torogai's mouth, which had been clamped in a stern line, softened slightly. Seeing this, Shuga added, as if it had just occurred to him, "I also have a request. Will you teach me the knowledge of the Yakoo in which Master Star Reader Nanai was so interested?"

Torogai's eyes widened. "Well now, that's an interesting thing for a Star Reader to say. It's a deal, if you'll teach me about Tendo in return."

It was Shuga's turn to look surprised. "You still want to learn new things even at your age?"

"Of course! But you'd better be careful. If anyone finds out you're interested in Yakoo lore, you'll never get to be Master Star Reader. Be clever about it. And if you want to learn about the Yakoo, then you'll have to let me go unharmed." She cackled. "Making up stories is your strong point, right? I'm counting on you to come up with a good story that doesn't hurt the prince's reputation but still includes us. This won't wait until you're Master Star Reader, either, so you'd better get cracking."

Shuga stared at her silently for a moment and then nodded. "I'll do my best," he said.

CHAPTER VII
A DREAM OF CLOUDS

After Torogai and Mon left, Balsa and the others went to the Aoyumi River and tried to decide whether Chagum had gone upstream or downstream. Mist no longer drifted along the river beach, which was growing dim in the twilight.

"I thought you said that after it's born, Nyunga Ro Im grows up in the sea. If that's true, wouldn't it make sense for Chagum to follow the river down to its mouth?" Balsa asked.

Tanda started to nod when his eyes were caught by something on the dry, rocky riverbed. "Is that the remains of a campfire?"

Balsa peered between the rocks and said impatiently, "Yes, but so what? Chagum couldn't have lit it, so shouldn't we be . . ." But he ignored her and ran over to it. Crouching down, he stared at it fixedly and showed no sign of budging.

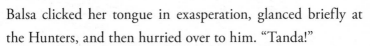

Balsa clicked her tongue in exasperation, glanced briefly at the Hunters, and then hurried over to him. "Tanda!"

He looked up at her slowly. "Balsa, I know where he's gone. He's heading for Sahnan."

"Sahnan?"

Tanda brushed the dirt from his knees and stood up. "The head of the Aoyumi River. 'Sahnan' means 'water's source' in Yakoo. The Yakoo always draw water from Sahnan for the midsummer festival, so this fire was set by villagers traveling upstream to get it. See? They've thrown salt on the fire to purify it." His gaze slowly sharpened, focusing on something no one else could see. "Fire! The midsummer festival! Damn!"

The glare he fixed then on Balsa and the men behind her was so fierce he seemed like a different person. "What a fool I've been! Earth is stronger than water, fire is stronger than earth — it's the most basic rule of magic weaving. Nyunga Ro Im is the Water Guardian, so its eggs are vulnerable to the earth spirit, Rarunga. And Rarunga's weakness must therefore be fire! Damn! Torogai and I thought that the midsummer festival had been completely changed by the first Mikado. That blinded us to the truth. Why do you think they use torches in the midsummer festival? The way they swing them at the demon is a symbol of how they defeated Rarunga!"

"Ah!" his three listeners exclaimed in unison. A vision of

the drama reenacted throughout the land during the mid-summer festival flashed through their minds: the wildly dancing water demon; the four men surrounding it, whirling their torches in the air; the hero portraying Mikado Torugaru, slaying the cornered demon with a final blow.

"In the legend of Torugaru, the water demon is destroyed at a spring." Tanda looked back at the forest where they had been attacked by Rarunga and pointed. "If Chagum inten-ded to go to the river's mouth, he would have gone that way when he came out of the forest. But Balsa, the path you took when you followed him leads this way." His finger traced the route until it pointed straight upstream. "To the river's source. Sahnan."

They strode off in the direction he indicated and kept moving even after the sun set and the river was enveloped in darkness. The moon, which was almost full, lit up the river so brightly that walking presented no difficulty for the travelers. Halfway through the night, however, they left the chilly river and went a short distance into the forest to light a fire and set up camp. Tanda insisted that if they were to be ready to fight, they needed to rest rather than to press recklessly onward; and despite their haste, they knew he was right.

Balsa broke branches and fed them to the fire. Although it was summer, nights in the mountains were still cold. "We're an odd bunch, aren't we?" she remarked, looking at the men around the fire. Jin and Zen chewed their dried meat wordlessly. Both had once fought her for their lives, and she had expected them to feel some bitterness toward her, yet she could detect no animosity in their expressions.

Jin swallowed his mouthful and looked at Tanda. "What are you? You look like you have Yakoo blood. Are you a magic weaver like that Torogai?"

"I'm just an apprentice — a petty magic weaver. My name is Tanda. And, as I'm sure you already know, this intimidating spear-woman is Balsa."

"We never really introduced ourselves, did we? My name's Jin, and this is Zen."

Tanda burst out laughing. "What? You mean your names are the numbers two and three?"

Jin smiled wryly. "That's because we're Hunters at the moment. Those are the names we use for now." He hesitated and then added, "If you hadn't pushed me out of the way, I'd have been killed by Rarunga's claws. I owe you my life."

Tanda looked taken aback, but then he nodded and said, "Don't mention it. I didn't even know it was you I was pushing."

Jin's smile widened. "I'll repay you someday," he said. "But if you're a magic weaver, does that mean you could see what that monster looked like?"

Tanda's face clouded. "Yes, I saw it, just for a second. It looked like a cross between a spider and a sea anemone — six legs, six giant claws on its back, a mouth filled with tentacles like whips. It was enormous, but it swam through the mud amazingly fast."

"How do you think it found Chagum?" Balsa asked. Jin and Zen were visibly startled to hear her say the prince's name without his title, but she ignored them. "It definitely tracked him down and attacked him, but it didn't notice when he got up in the trees and made his way to the river. Do you think it makes a difference if his feet are actually touching the ground?"

"I bet that's it. Rarunga is an earth spirit. From the way it moved, it's probably pretty agile in soil or mud, but I think it would be difficult for it to travel over hard surfaces like rock. You said a mist covered the water after Chagum dived in the river, right? If the egg is in control of his body, then it's probably using water to escape from Rarunga. But even if we use fire, Rarunga can hide in Nayugu. It would be easy if we could attack it in that other world, but not even we magic weavers can do that. I have no idea what will happen at the spring. I just know we have to find a way to protect Chagum. . . ."

"You told us that it has a mouth," Balsa said, "so it will have to come here if it wants to eat him. We'll just have to attack it when it shows itself."

"But there's no guarantee of that. It could just grab him with its tentacles and vanish into Nayugu."

Their conversation continued late into the night.

As Balsa, Jin, and Zen were all experts in combat and warfare, the ideas flew. They discussed the best ways to use fire and exploit it to their advantage. Finally their talk began to slow, and Tanda rubbed his face. The stubble on his chin made a rasping sound. "What an awful day! I'm so tired. You guys sure are tough. Do you mind if I go to bed?"

Balsa smiled. "Go ahead. We'll take turns sleeping. Tiredness can cost you your life." She took the first watch, and the others lay down on the ground, wrapped up in sheets of oiled paper. They were instantly asleep.

Although they had not been talking loudly, everything suddenly seemed very still. A breeze passed by, rustling the branches overhead. Through them, Balsa glimpsed the moon shining brightly in the indigo sky. Somewhere, its light must be shining on Chagum too.

She wondered if he was lonely. She sighed and moved over to lean her back against a tree trunk. It was hard to believe that only eight months had passed since she met him last fall. Gently, she rubbed her face. Her hand felt cold.

Once, a long time ago, she had loved her mother and her father, and she had loved Jiguro. Now those whom she had loved so deeply were gone. She looked over at Tanda's sleeping form and recalled Chagum's face — never tanned by the sun and still a little childlike. She heaved another deep sigh.

Chagum had long since left the Aoyumi River, walking beside it through the dark woods. And yet he kept to the water, *in* the water, for in Nayugu, the place where he walked was still a river; one so broad that he could not see the opposite bank and so deep that he could not see the bottom. He moved in a dream, seeing the worlds of Sagu and Nayugu simultaneously, his feet automatically evading the stones and roots in Sagu while he watched the fish of Nayugu swim among the trees. The ground beneath his feet was transparent, and the water — a breathtaking clear blue — dropped down into a darkness no light could penetrate.

He continued walking through this clear, silent landscape. Far to the right, the riverbank in Nayugu gradually came into view. Crystal waters lapped against the white shore, and blue-green waterweeds waved between the tree roots of Sagu. Suddenly, he noticed something floating toward him, weaving like a snake as it rose from the abyss at his feet. Its hair was like seaweed, its skin smooth and slippery, its eyes and mouth those of a fish . . . A voice poured from its mouth and, carried by the water, resounded in his mind.

> *"Nyunga Ro Chaga,*
> *O Guardian of the Spirit.*
> *Not long now, not long.*
> *When the sun sets and rises again,*
> *then will it be time for the birthing."*

The creature swam and swirled around him joyfully. Many more Yona Ro Gai gathered, rising from deep beneath him in all directions. They beat their webbed hands on the water's surface, spraying drops that shimmered against the transparent ground of Sagu.

> *"O egg embraced by Nyunga Ro Chaga!*
> *Become Nyunga Ro Im.*
> *Breathe clouds and make the sweet rain fall*
> *on this land and that other land."*

They continued to circle around Chagum until the sun set and the river was wrapped in darkness. When the night deepened, he lay down on the thick ferns beneath a great tree. Lights rose like fireflies from the depths, drifting to the water's surface, clustering together and suddenly scattering. He watched them dance, and before he knew it, he had fallen asleep.

That night, his dreams merged with those of Nyunga Ro Im as the egg dozed, waiting to be born. This was Nyunga Ro Im's only gift for the one in whom its egg resided: the dream of the cloud spirit, which none but its Guardian could ever hope to see. In the dream, Chagum was an enormous shellfish, larger than the palace in the capital, lying on his belly at the bottom of the great river. He watched the world from a hard shell that radiated seven colors of light. The earth's energy seeped inside him, circulated warmly through his stomach, and filled his entire being.

Myriad lives — all life on the peninsula — flowed like a

shining, swirling river in and out of his dream. Strong lives, weak lives, from both Sagu and Nayugu: Some were fortunate, protected by many others, while some wandered into blind creeks, petered out, and vanished soon after they were born. His body nestled into this great flowing river. *Ahhh.* Like a great sigh, he exhaled the energy flowing inside him and let his mind ride that breath as it rushed to the surface, burst from the water, and climbed up, up to the heavens. . . .

In the blue sky, his breath became a cloud, and he gazed from a dazzling height upon the clear blue river and the world through which it wound. The wind pushed against him, passing out the other side, and birds glided gently through him. He merged with clouds that drifted toward him from far away, smelled the scents of different lands, whirled and swelled. . . . Light was born within him, and with a flash of lightning and a clap of thunder, he became a drop of rain and fell once again to the bottom of the river.

Sensing the pale blue dawn, Chagum awoke and knew that all was ready. The egg within his breast ached. It was time to be born.

The morning sun shone through the green canopy covering the sky and cast a dappled light on the ferns and bamboo grass beneath.

"Wait."

Balsa, who had been rushing ahead, stopped at the sound of Jin's voice behind her. He was crouching down, staring at the ferns at the foot of a huge tree. "What is it?"

Jin raised his head. "It looks like Tanda was right. Someone seems to have slept here. From the state of these ferns, whoever it was left about dawn."

Zen was standing beside him. He pointed to the ground and said quietly, "It was the prince. There's no mistake. Look — a footprint."

Balsa pushed her way back through the underbrush and looked at the ground where he was pointing. The imprint of a small straw sandal was faintly visible, and the marks of two thin ropes across the sole stood out particularly clearly. She felt her heart constrict. "Yes, that's Chagum's footprint all right. I can see the marks from the straw ropes I added to keep him from slipping." She stood up and looked at Tanda. "How far is it to the spring?"

"About two hours at our pace."

"If he left at dawn, he'll reach the spring at least half an hour ahead of us. If we add how long it will take to make torches, we don't have a moment to spare." Balsa looked at Jin and Zen and smiled challengingly. "Now's your chance to prove what you're worth."

The Hunters just grinned back.

CHAPTER VIII
THE WIND OF SAHNAN
AND THE WINGS OF THE *NAHJI*

As if the egg were pulling him, Chagum headed straight
for the spring. He moved out of the forest down to the river
beach and kept on walking as fast as his body would allow.
The sun rose and its strong rays beat steadily on the back of
his neck, but he did not even feel the summer heat. When
the river had dwindled to little more than a stream and he
was almost in sight of the spring, he stopped abruptly.

The world around him, which had been nothing more
than a vague dream, came sharply into focus; his body, sensing mortal danger, yanked him out of the dream of Nyunga
Ro Im, and he broke into a sweat, the cold slimy sweat of
fear. Through the pleasant scene of the river beach in Sagu,
he saw before him in Nayugu a huge sea of mud, as if all the
water in an enormous lake had dried up, leaving the muddy
bottom exposed in all directions. One small patch of grass

perched like a floating island in the middle — the river's source in the land of Sagu. At its center, he could see a large black hole, with the invisible energy of the earth rising out of it. Chagum knew instinctively that this energy was the very thing the egg needed to complete its growth.

But he could smell only death — the stench of Rarunga, the Egg Eater — and he began to tremble with fear. His stomach tightened and his heart pounded wildly in his chest. His foot jerked. He shuddered and froze, trying to stop it from moving. The egg was urging his body forward, pushing him on, but he reeked of *shigu salua*. If he set one foot out of the water on that sea of mud, Rarunga was sure to smell it and come after him — to rive his body with its enormous claws and eat the egg!

NO! I don't want to die! But his foot inched forward. Shaking, he fought with all his might to pull it back, but like a baby about to be born, bathed in its mother's blood, the egg was already straining toward life, desperate to outstrip death in its race against time. Chagum could not hope to suppress that primal urge. The egg seemed to burn within him, and again, he felt his foot dragged slowly forward.

Responding to the terror that gripped the cloud spirit and Chagum, a white mist began to rise slowly above the surface of the river. The water became thick as syrup and gave off a faint metallic odor — the scent of their fear. Chagum's foot began to move again, and this time he could not stop it. Like a fish seeking air, he raised his head and screamed: "Balsa!"

"It's just a little farther to Sahnan," Tanda muttered, then stopped abruptly.

Balsa looked back at him. "What's wrong?" she demanded.

"Shh!" Tanda crouched down beside the Aoyumi River, putting his face so close to the water he almost touched it. He had heard the call of the Yona Ro Gai, the Water Dwellers of Nayugu. Chanting a spell, he opened his eyes to that other world —

— and gasped in surprise. He was floating on the surface of a great winding river. The riverbank rose in the direction of Sahnan, but beyond that, he realized with shock, there was only a great sea of mud ringed by mountains — the Egg Eater's nest! And Chagum must pass through it for the egg to be born. . . .

Tanda saw several strange creatures swimming toward him — the Yona Ro Gai. "Young To Ro Gai, Land Dweller of Sagu." Tanda struggled to breathe as he listened. "To Ro Gai the Elder sends you this message. 'Do not just make torches. Drench them in oil to make a fire that cannot be quenched by water, and fight Rarunga. Take the egg and thro —'"

But Tanda could stand it no more. He drew in a deep, whistling breath and collapsed face up on the ground in Sagu.

"Tanda! What's going on?" Balsa cried. She helped him to a sitting position.

Through a fit of coughing, he said, "Torogai sent us a message through the Yona Ro Gai. She said, don't just make torches. Drench them in oil so they can't be quenched by water . . . We don't have time! We've got to hurry and pour oil inside the torches." Tanda fixed his eyes on Balsa. "In Nayugu, Sahnan is a sea of mud."

At that moment, they heard a faint scream. Balsa jumped to her feet and set off at a run.

"Balsa! Wait! Are you planning to fight Rarunga without a torch?" Tanda shouted, but she had already vaulted over the rocks and disappeared toward the spring. He frantically stopped the Hunters who had started after her. "Wait! Don't go yet! We've got to ready the torches first. I'm sure Balsa will buy us enough time for that."

Balsa raced into the river mist — the same mist she had seen before. The dense white fog limited her vision, but she could still make out a small shape running ahead of her: *Chagum.* She had almost caught up with him at last.

But suddenly she felt a deadly malice course through her body, oozing through the ground under her feet just as it had before. Right as Chagum neared the spring, huge claws ripped their way through the earth, surrounding him on every side.

I'll never make it in time! Balsa clenched her teeth.

And yet the claws moved ever so slowly, as if they were cutting through rock. *The egg . . . It changed the water from*

the spring! When she realized this, Balsa jumped onto the river; it was firmer than ice, a road glowing with a pale blue light, and she raced forward as fast as she could. But the claws could still break through it, and with loud cracking noises, they closed slowly, inexorably, upon the frozen Chagum.

But Chagum was no longer scared. Although he could see the terrible Rarunga, he was looking at Nayugu, at the floating island beneath his feet. While his calm was partly due to the egg's desire to be born, it mostly came from Chagum himself, his deep internal will to survive.

He felt the egg inside him begin to move, rising from his chest to his throat, his throat to his mouth. Before him lay the hole, a deep, deep pit from which the earth's breath rose. Instinctively, Chagum crouched down on all fours, looking down into Sahnan, urged by the egg into the position that would allow it to be born in Nayugu.

Whoosh! A warm, moist gust of energy wafted upward. This was where the sacred life force of Sagu and Nayugu merged together and rose to the heavens. Exposed to such concentrated energy, the egg completed its final stage of growth, its shell hardening to protect it in both worlds. *Hurry! Hurry! Hurry!* Chagum thought, and as if it were responding to his urgency, the egg slipped into his mouth.

At that very moment Balsa reached his side. Rarunga's claws cast their long, sharp shadows over them; there was no time to think. She bent over Chagum, wrapped her left arm around his body, and tried to pick him up. He kicked out and twisted frantically in her arms, fighting to stay near Sahnan. While they struggled, Rarunga's claws closed tighter, until Balsa realized their opening was gone. Filled with a premonition of death, she hugged Chagum tightly, feeling the warmth of his body against her.

Chagum opened his mouth — and as he did so, the invisible egg dropped from his mouth into the world of Nayugu. Instantly, Rarunga vanished from Sagu to find the egg in that other world. Down the egg fell, deep into the hole of Nayugu. Then, as if the earth had exhaled suddenly, a blast of energy rushed up from the bottom, caught the egg, and carried it, revolving and dancing, up into the sky. Rarunga's tentacles reached out to grab it, but just before they touched it, the egg left Nayugu.

Balsa had no idea what was going on, but she did not waste the precious time afforded by the monster's disappearance. She tightened her hold on Chagum and picked him up. A blue light appeared in front of her at the very instant she sensed Rarunga's return. As Chagum grasped the egg, which danced in the light of the energy from the hole, Balsa leapt into the air and Rarunga erupted from the ground beneath her. Still carrying Chagum, who now clutched the egg, Balsa shot between the claws that surrounded them like a cage. Tentacles whipped after them, chasing the elusive egg.

Balsa flipped in midair and swung her spear with lightning speed, pinning the end of a tentacle to the ground. A voiceless shriek resounded, shaking the earth. She stepped on the tentacle and pulled out her spear before the next one could reach her. But in that brief moment, claws ripped up through the ground beneath, aiming straight for them. There was no time to escape. Balsa jumped onto a claw, clamping its hard shell sides between her feet, and used its upward momentum to propel herself into the air. Somersaulting, she whirled Chagum by his belt and let him go just before she landed, throwing him clear of Rarunga's claws. All of this she did without thinking, her body reacting instinctively.

The instant she let go, she regretted it: If he hit a rock, it would kill him. But the training that Balsa had given him saved Chagum's life. As he landed on the roots of a tree, he rolled his body into a ball, protecting his head and absorbing the shock of impact with his shoulder and hips. Balsa ran toward him, dodging the tentacles that came snaking through the air like whips and knocking them aside with her spear.

Suddenly, a tentacle snagged her foot and slammed her hard against the ground, then with a vicelike grip, it raised her dangling into the air. A shining claw, keen as a sword, raced toward her. The tentacle swung her high, clearly intending to smash her against the claw, and she could do nothing to stop it.

She gritted her teeth, waiting for the blow, when suddenly the tentacle jerked violently. The point of the claw passed beneath her shoulder, and she felt a burning pain cross her back. Twisting around, she caught sight of someone wielding a torch — Jin! He pressed the blazing brand against the tentacle, billowing dense black smoke in every direction. Tanda and Zen stood behind him, guarding his back.

A horrible stench enveloped Balsa, and with a shriek that rent the air, Rarunga threw her into space. She tucked her knees up and curled herself into a ball, somersaulting twice in the air. Hitting the ground in a spray of gravel, she rolled sideways and flipped herself upright immediately. Her clothes had been slashed open and a deep gash ran down her back, yet the wound barely bled, and she felt no pain. Battle fever seized her, stronger than anything she had ever experienced before.

Behind her, Tanda and the others swung their torches, pressing the flames against Rarunga's claws and tentacles. But they knew it was next to impossible to destroy the monster with torches alone; whenever it felt the sizzling heat, it vanished into Nayugu, only to reappear in Sagu and attack from a different direction. Still Tanda and Jin and Zen fought on. Drenched in sweat, the three torchbearers looked like they were dancing, but it was a dance on which their very lives depended; one slip, and they would die.

And all the while, the tentacles, which were highly sensitive to smell, kept searching for the egg of Nyunga Ro Im. Dodging the flames, they groped along the ground, sniffing out the scent that drove Rarunga, whetting its appetite. At last, they found Chagum, curled up at the base of a tree.

Although Chagum had not hit his head when he slammed into the tree, the shock had left him stunned. His mind only cleared when Balsa reached his side, slipped her arm around him, and picked him up. He had been afraid that he had squashed the egg, but it was unharmed, glowing with a bluish light in his right palm. It was as hard and smooth as a stone, and he could feel its faint warmth: It felt alive.

Balsa saw the egg. "Chagum! Get rid of that thing! Throw it away! Hurry!"

He looked up at her wide-eyed. *If I throw it away, I'll be saved*, he thought. *So will Tanda and the others. What's the point in protecting it if we give up our lives?* But many other thoughts flashed through his mind as well: the egg's warmth, its helplessness. It no longer had any power over him; it could not even communicate its urgent desire to live. It could only sit there silently, gently warming his palm. Yet, to him, that desire was still painfully clear. It had chosen him, believed in him, entrusted its life to him, just because it so desperately wanted to live.

His thoughts were interrupted by rage — a murderous rage that came from outside him, spilling from the ground and numbing his entire being. As Balsa made to escape with him in her arms, Chagum pushed his feet against the tree roots and slipped from her grasp. "Chagum!" she screamed. The ground split open like a ripe pomegranate, and Rarunga's claws appeared.

Tanda saw Chagum racing toward him, the claws

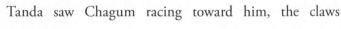

suddenly rearing up behind. Yet his mind was distracted by a shrill cry — a flock of birds flying toward them. *"Kaw-oh! Kaw-oh!"* A light flashed on in his brain. *Nahji . . . The nahji!* The warding charm made of *nahji* bones at the edge of the village; the midsummer festival song; the *nahji* that flew faster than the devil. . . . Suddenly he knew exactly what they must do. "Chagum!" he yelled, running toward him. "The *nahji*! The *nahji*! Throw the egg up into the air!"

Tentacles sped whining toward Chagum. One almost touched him, but Balsa, behind him, grabbed it and wrestled it to the ground. Yet another whipped toward him. Jin and Zen ran to his aid, but they could not stop it from latching onto Chagum's right arm, yanking it with sudden and dreadful force. With a sickening sound, a sharp pain shot through his right shoulder; it had been dislocated.

The tentacle arched backward, pulling Chagum up into the air, and its tip slithered toward the egg in his hand. The fine hairs of the tip fanned open to reveal a sucker. Screaming, Chagum tried desperately to grasp the egg with his left hand, but with his right arm held high by the tentacle, he could only dangle limply from his injured shoulder. Just as he was about to give up, a large hand reached up beside him and snatched the egg from him. Looking at its owner, Chagum forgot his pain and his face brightened. "Tanda!"

Tanda threw the egg into the heavens as if loosing an arrow from its bow. One bird separated from the flock of *nahji* flying south across the Misty Blue Mountains. Through a blur of tears, Chagum watched it dart downward, glide smoothly toward the egg, and grasp it, still glowing, in its beak. Swiftly it sped across the sky and vanished from sight. The egg had finally escaped Rarunga's clutches.

It had disappeared so quickly, however, that Rarunga could not follow its scent, and its attention focused on Chagum, who still smelled strongly of the egg. Tanda grabbed him with his right arm and pressed the flaming torch in his left hand against the tentacle that gripped him. With a bloodcurdling scream, the monster released its hold, but instantly, other tentacles swarmed toward Chagum, clinging to him like leeches to their prey. The torch flew out of Tanda's grasp, and he and Chagum were

swept up into the air.

"Chagum! Tanda!" Balsa stabbed at the four tentacles that held them. Her spear moved with such ferocious speed that it was almost invisible. Jin and Zen jumped inside the ring of claws, using their torches to protect her as the circle tightened. Fluid oozed from the holes Balsa had gouged in the tentacles, and Rarunga writhed in agony: Fire was anathema to a creature accustomed to living in the cold, dark mud.

Balsa felt the ground buck and heave beneath her. Suddenly, the enormous, slimy body of the monster emerged from the earth, spraying clods of dirt. Balsa, Jin, and Zen were thrown back off their feet. The creature's giant mouth gaped inside the circle of claws crowning the body, and the tentacles shoved their captives relentlessly toward it.

Yelling, Jin and Zen threw their torches at its mouth, but the tentacles surrounding the opening knocked them aside. Tanda's leg was already inside Rarunga's mouth. Balsa ran over and picked up the torch he had dropped. With the torch in her right hand and her spear in her left, she leapt into the air and threw her spear with all her might. Using the momentum of that swing, she immediately sent the torch flying after it.

The torch followed the path of the spear perfectly. The tentacles knocked the spear aside, leaving a brief opening for the torch. It sailed past Tanda's leg and with a horrible, sizzling sound lodged itself firmly in the monster's mouth. With a wordless scream, Rarunga threw its captives high into the air and vanished. Chagum and Tanda slammed into the ground with a sickening thud, and then there was silence.

With a sound like a sigh, the stream resumed its quiet burbling. Balsa ran to Chagum where he lay on the riverbank and lifted him up. His face was deathly pale and covered in a sheen of sweat. His eyelids fluttered. Dazed, he opened them and looked up at her, his eyes unfocused. "My . . . arm . . . hurts."

Balsa breathed a deep sigh of relief and cradled his head in her arms.

C H A P T E R   I X
A DIFFERENT DESTINY

On midsummer's day, they camped a little way from the spring. Tanda fixed Chagum's dislocated shoulder, immobilizing it in a makeshift sling, then rubbed a strong-smelling ointment on his side, where he had bruised it when Rarunga flung him onto the riverbank.

"I outdid myself, didn't I?" Balsa said with a laugh as Tanda treated the cut on her back.

Tanda snorted. "We all did."

They heard Jin's voice and looked up to see the Hunters returning with two plump pheasants and several dormice for their meal. Noticing that Chagum was awake, Jin and Zen knelt before him, trembling, their heads bowed low. "Your Highness!" They could not look him in the eye.

Chagum frowned. "I'm no longer a prince," he muttered. "So there's no need to treat me like one." *I wish that I could ask them what my father's orders were*, he thought suddenly. *Did he really tell them to kill me?* But this thought was gradually replaced by the feeling that it did not matter anymore. He was deeply tired, not only in body but in his very soul.

The birds the Hunters caught had been tossed casually on the ground. His glance fell upon their lifeless carcasses, and a shudder ran through him. Tanda, who was holding his wrist to take his pulse, followed his gaze. "To eat or be eaten, to escape or be taken," he whispered and then looked at Chagum. "A matter of utmost importance to the one concerned, yet it happens all the time and we don't even notice."

Chagum's eyes filled with tears. Balsa wrapped her arm around his shoulder and whispered, "I'm so glad you survived. I'm so glad we made it in time."

Her words filled his heart with a warmth that spread to every corner of his body. *I didn't "survive,"* he thought. *You saved me.* This realization hit him forcefully. Even he, who had known firsthand the egg's desire to live, had found it hard to sacrifice himself to save it. Yet these people had willingly confronted terror for his sake. As a prince, he had taken it for granted that he should be protected, but now he knew how precious this protection was. He wrapped his good arm around Balsa's neck and hugged her tightly.

"Thank you," he said. He could find no other words to say. He looked at Tanda, then at the Hunters, and said again, "Thank you." At that moment, the tension that had gripped him for the last eight months finally melted away. *It's over*, he thought.

Neither he nor Balsa could know that another fate was quietly but surely approaching.

The next morning, they slept to their heart's content and only put out the fire and set off on their journey once the sun had fully risen. To their surprise, they were met a little before noon by a troop of soldiers climbing up the mountain path. Torogai walked in front, and her face brightened at the sight of Balsa and her companions.

Jin and Zen hurried over to Mon, who led the soldiers, and told him what had happened the previous day. For a brief moment, Mon's face was suffused with deep joy, but at the sight of Chagum approaching, he prostrated himself on the ground. With a clanking of armor, the other soldiers followed suit. Mon, who had shed his role as head of the Hunters and resumed his role as a member of the palace guard, addressed Chagum with downcast eyes.

"I beg your leave to express our joy that we have found you safe and well," he said formally. "How profound is our gratitude that you have saved the water god and thereby delivered our country from drought. It is a great honor to witness the return of our sacred founder, Torugaru. The tale of your glorious heroism will be told for generations to come, Your Highness, Crown Prince."

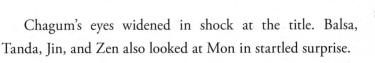

Chagum's eyes widened in shock at the title. Balsa, Tanda, Jin, and Zen also looked at Mon in startled surprise.

"Did you address me as the Crown Prince?" Chagum automatically slipped into the commanding tones of royalty.

"Yes, Your Highness. I am afraid that I am the bearer of sad tidings. The night before last, your illustrious brother, the Crown Prince Sagum, passed away from illness. The Mikado has officially declared the Second Prince, Chagum, to be the next Crown Prince and heir to the throne. While, to our great regret, we were unable to protect you previously, we stand ready now to accompany Your Highness to the palace."

Chagum felt a profound sorrow rise from deep in his heart. It was not grief at his brother's death; they had been raised separately, and the few times they met, Sagum had treated him with disdain. Chagum had never thought of him as anything but a stranger. But with his death, a new destiny fastened itself around him like a cloak of steel, tightening inexorably. Thoughts and feelings raced through his mind. *I can see my mother . . . This means that someday I will be the Mikado.* But for some reason everything seemed cold and distant. His strongest, most immediate emotion was unbearable sadness.

He looked up at Balsa. She was gazing straight at him. To the soldiers' shock, the Crown Prince suddenly threw his arms around this grimy, bloodstained stranger and burst into tears, wailing as though his heart would break. "I don't want to go! I don't want to be the stupid Crown Prince! I want to stay with you and Tanda forever!" He hugged her fiercely. Balsa stood motionless, weeping soundlessly, tears streaking one after the other down her cheeks. Then, unable to restrain herself any longer, she suddenly scooped him up in her arms, hugged him tightly, and buried her face in his shoulder. She stood this way for a few moments, then slowly lowered him to the ground.

"Will you run away with me then, Chagum?" she said huskily. The soldiers tensed, and she laughed. "How about it? Shall I show them what I can do?"

Chagum looked up at her, hiccupping. He knew what she was trying to say. He stepped back from her slowly and looked at Tanda, then at Torogai. Knowing what Chagum must be going through, Tanda's face twisted sadly; it was such a cruel fate for a boy of only twelve to confront. But no one could help him. Tanda clenched his fists tightly.

Chagum closed his eyes and drew in a deep breath, trying to suppress his hiccups. The fragrance of the trees filled him, fresh and invigorating. He no longer smelled of *shigu salua*. No matter how hard he tried, he would never again see Nayugu. The egg of Nyunga Ro Im was gone. . . . He knew inside that a certain period of his life had ended. Through no desire of his own, he had become the Moribito, the Guardian of the Spirit; and so too he would now be made Crown Prince. He was furious with whatever it was that was moving him against his will, yet at the same time, he felt a strange clarity. It was similar to the feeling he had experienced in the wide, cool world of Nayugu, a feeling that would remain in his heart for the rest of his life.

He raised his eyes and, still hiccupping slightly, looked at Balsa. "It's all right," he said. "Save that for some other child." Then he grinned mischievously and added, "Maybe it will be yours and Tanda's."

Balsa and Tanda started in surprise. Torogai threw her head back and laughed heartily. "Well done, lad! Well done! You're brilliant. That's the way to tell them." When she had her laughter under control again, she added, "You're more mature than any of these adults here, that's for sure."

Her words made him very happy.

They continued down the mountain, following the Aoyumi River to the capital. Compared to their previous journey, it was a very peaceful trip, but their hearts were heavy. They camped twice on their way to the capital, and Chagum told Mon he wished to share his campfire with Balsa and her companions. He would permit only Jin, Zen, and Mon to join them. Mon bowed his head in assent.

Conversation around the campfire centered on Nyunga Ro Im and Rarunga. "Do you think that the *nahji* has already carried the egg to the sea?" Chagum asked.

Tanda nodded. "Yes. The *nahji*'s wings are strong. There's a Yakoo song that goes like this." He sang,

"In a single day, the nahji *flies*
from the Misty Blue Mountains to the sea.
Would that I had the wings of the nahji.*"*

"Tanda," Chagum exclaimed. "You have a good voice!"

"Don't be silly," Tanda said gruffly, blushing. If Chagum realized it was a love song, he would be bound to tease him again, and Tanda had had quite enough of that. But Chagum did not appear to notice.

"So the egg must be at the bottom of the sea by now," he continued. "I wonder when Nyunga Ro Im will hatch."

"I don't know," Balsa said, "but it better start producing clouds soon or this year's harvest will be a disaster. After all the trouble it caused us, it better do a good job as Nyunga Ro Im." Everyone nodded fervently.

"Do you think that Rarunga lives for hundreds of years?" Chagum asked. "And does it only eat Nyunga Ro Im's eggs?"

Torogai, who was lying on her side, her head pillowed on her arm, snorted. "Not likely. How could it survive if that's all it ate? It must live on something else instead. Those eggs are probably a special treat that it gets once a century. Still, I don't know for sure — I never even found out how Nyunga Ro Im got that egg inside you. Who knows? Maybe the Nyunga Ro Im that lays its eggs every hundred years in Sagu only exists on this peninsula, and there are other Nyunga Ro Im that protect their eggs in different ways in other parts of the world."

Chagum's expression suddenly grew serious. He looked at Torogai and said, "I think I know why Nyunga Ro Im picked me."

Torogai sat up abruptly. "Really?"

"Well, I can't say for certain. But while the egg was guiding me to the spring, I had a dream — a very strange dream. I think I must have seen what the soul of Nyunga Ro Im was dreaming." Searching for words, he haltingly described the river of life that he had felt flowing through him. "Maybe Nyunga Ro Im chose me because it saw that I was protected by so many other lives. It must have felt that my life was the strongest, one that would protect the egg and give it the best chance of surviving. . . . But I don't know how it laid the egg inside me."

243

Torogai pondered this for a while and then nodded. "I see. Hmm. You might be right. Previous Guardians must have been in similar positions or had similar strength. You know, we Yakoo believe that children of eleven or twelve have the strongest life force. The souls of children under seven are not yet firmly rooted in this world, and so they die easily. And at the age of fourteen or fifteen, people's bodies are preparing to give birth to the next generation, and their energy is channeled into that. Maybe Nyunga Ro Im's egg is planted by the rain or something, but regardless of how it does it, the spirit picks a child with a strong life force to guard it. Of course, this is just a guess." She sighed, threw herself onto her back, and stretched out her arms and legs. "Oh, dear. I've lived seventy years and there's still so much I don't know about this world! Drat! The heavens and earth turn so slowly, as if they didn't care. Hey, you there, you good-for-nothing apprentice! You'd better give up the idea of being a magic weaver. Nothing could be more frustrating!"

Tanda smiled wryly. "Don't worry," he said. "It will take me at least another fifty years to come to that realization. I'll stick with it a little longer."

Mon and Jin exchanged glances. They had never dreamed that they would one day be sitting around a campfire with people like this. Just as Torogai and her companions lived in their own world, so Jin and Mon were bound to a world that would not let them go, one to which they would return as soon as they entered the capital tomorrow.

Balsa nudged Chagum and pointed upward. The night sky, so high it seemed it would swallow them, was spangled with stars that looked like silver grains of sand. Until a moment ago, it had been clear, but now a wisp of cloud scudded across it, slender and delicate as a breath on a snowy morning.

At evening on the following day, they reached Yamakage Bridge, which only the royal family and their retainers could cross. Balsa and her companions stopped at the foot of the bridge and watched an ox-drawn carriage pull up in front of Chagum. He turned and looked back at Balsa.

"Balsa," he said, "Call me Chagum. Say 'Farewell, Chagum.'"

Balsa smiled faintly. "Farewell, Chagum," she said.

He clenched his teeth. "Thank you. And good-bye. Balsa, Tanda, Master Torogai . . . Thank you."

Then he turned abruptly and bent his head to climb into the carriage. It rolled forward, the sound of its wheels echoing in the valley below. The summer sun flashed on its fittings as it slowly disappeared into the golden light of sunset.

EPILOGUE
IN THE RAIN

The drops fell incessantly, like fine threads of silver trailing from the heavy, low-lying clouds. Cloaked in a straw cape and hat, Balsa strode through the rain, carrying her spear bundled in oiled paper. She intended to cross the Misty Blue Mountains before autumn and enter the kingdom of Kanbal.

She thought back to her conversation with Tanda after they had parted from Chagum, and the expression on his face when she told him that she planned to set off for Kanbal immediately. "I need a little time," she said then, groping for words. "Time to think. I've avoided this for many years, but now I'm ready to go back. I want to find Jiguro's friends and family to tell them what happened, what kind of life he lived." She gazed at the other side of the bridge where Chagum had disappeared. "I think that after meeting

Chagum and serving as his bodyguard, I can finally understand how Jiguro felt. That's why, you see."

She turned her gaze back to Tanda. He was smiling faintly. "I'm glad to hear it. Off you go then, to Kanbal. But don't go wielding that spear of yours over there. There may be better men than me in Kanbal, but I doubt there are any who will sew up your wounds for free."

Balsa laughed out loud. And so they had parted.

As she listened to the patter of the rain on the leaves above her head, she felt the aching void of Chagum's absence at her side. They had not even spent a year together, yet she had so many memories of him. . . . As she walked, she recalled, one by one, all the things that had happened since she had leapt into the Aoyumi River and dragged his body to shore.

I wonder what he's doing now, she thought. *What kind of life will he lead?* She felt a sharp pang at the thought that she would not be a part of it. *We'll probably never meet again.* The boy that she had met so suddenly and parted from just as abruptly would spend the rest of his life within the palace, the son of a god descended from heaven. . . . *In the end, all I could do was to help save his life.* Yet perhaps the day would come when he would remember her with the same feeling she held for her foster father, Jiguro.

Rain streamed from the edge of her straw hat.

The world around her could change so suddenly, for no apparent reason. She could only do her best to live with those changes, seeking, as everyone must, the path in life that was right for her. There was surely no such thing as a life without any regrets at all.

Ah, how I'd love some of Tanda's vegetable stew, she thought. She smiled. Through the trees in the valley, she could glimpse, far in the distance, blue mountains shrouded in rain.

THE END

LIST OF
CHARACTERS

BALSA an itinerant female bodyguard and skilled spear-wielder from Kanbal

CHAGUM the Second Prince of New Yogo

GAKAI a Star Reader

JIGURO MUSA Balsa's foster father, the strongest spear-wielder in Kanbal

JIN a Hunter; the name means "Two"

KAINAN NANAI the first Master Star Reader

KARUNA YONSA Balsa's father, the physician to the king of Kanbal

THE MASTER STAR READER the Mikado's closest advisor, who functions as the prime minister; the real name of the current Master Star Reader is Hibi Tonan

THE MIKADO the ruler of New Yogo; Chagum's father

MON the leader of the Hunters; the name means "One"

NAGURU onetime king of Kanbal

NINA a little girl of Yakoo descent

NOYA a man of Yakoo descent; Nina's grandfather

ROGSAM onetime king of Kanbal

SAGUM the Crown Prince of New Yogo

SAYA a young girl who was once saved by Balsa; lives with Toya in Ogi no Shimo

THE SECOND QUEEN Chagum's mother

SHUGA a Star Reader

SIGURU a Yakoo boy who once served as the Guardian of the Spirit

SUNE a Hunter; the name means "Eight"

TAGA a Hunter; the name means "Seven"

TANDA a healer and apprentice magic weaver; Balsa's childhood friend

TOROGAI one of the greatest magic weavers of that time

TORUGARU the first Mikado and founder of New Yogo

TOYA an errand runner in Kosenkyo, who was once saved by Balsa; lives with Saya in Ogi no Shimo

YUGA a man of Yakoo descent who lives in the village of Yashiro; Nina's father

YUN a Hunter; the name means "Four"

ZEN a Hunter; the name means "Three"

LIST OF
PLACES & TERMS

AOIKE POND a pond on the Nayoro Peninsula, where *shigu salua* grows

AOYUMI RIVER a river that runs just outside Kosenkyo

HOSHINOMIYA PALACE also known as the Star Palace; home to and headquarters of the Star Readers

ICHINOMIYA PALACE home of the First Prince

JUCHI RO GAI the Mud Dwellers of Nayugu

KANBAL a country north of New Yogo, over the Misty Blue Mountains

KOSENKYO capital of New Yogo; the name means "shining fan"

MORIBITO the Yogoese name for the Guardian of the Spirit

NAHJI a bird sacred to the Yakoo

NAYORO PENINSULA where the action takes place

NAYUGU to the Yakoo, a world that overlaps with Sagu. Although normally Nayugu is invisible to people in Sagu, the two interact and affect one another.

NEW YOGO the country on the Nayoro Peninsula founded by Torugaru and Nanai

NINOMIYA PALACE home of the Second Prince

NYUNGA RO CHAGA the Yakoo name for the Guardian of the Spirit

NYUNGA RO IM the Yakoo name for the Water Spirit

OGI NO KAMI the royal district of Kosenkyo; the name means "the handle of the fan"

OGI NO NAKA the district of Kosenkyo where the nobility live; the name means "the center of the fan"

OGI NO SHIMO the district of Kosenkyo where the commoners live; the name means "the edge of the fan"

RARUNGA the Egg Eater; it dwells in Nayugu but can cross over to Sagu

SAGU to the Yakoo, the visible world, where humans live

SAHNAN head of the Aoyumi River; in Yakoo, "the water's source"

SANNOMIYA PALACE home of the Third Queen

SHIGU SALUA a kind of water plant with a distinctive flower and smell

SHURIKEN a sharp metal throwing dart

TEN NO KAMI the supreme god of the Yogoese

TENDO the Yogoese Law of the Universe

TO RO GAI the Land Dwellers of Sagu

TORINAKI RIVER a river that runs along the east side of Kosenkyo

YAKOO the indigenous people of the Nayoro Peninsula

YASHIRO a village in New Yogo where many Yakoo live

YOGO the people who colonized the Nayoro Peninsula; also, the country from which they came. The name means "land blessed by Ten no Kami."

YONA RO GAI the Water Dwellers of Nayugu

AUTHOR'S NOTE

Thirteen years ago, the idea for this story popped into my mind unexpectedly, like a little seed. I had borrowed some movies to watch at home, something I love to do in my spare time. I was just relaxing in the living room, not paying much attention to the previews, when suddenly a scene from an action movie caught my eye. I don't even remember what movie it was, but there was a burning bus and I saw a woman, just an extra in the movie, leading a child by the hand as they escaped from the fire.

Suddenly I wanted to write a story — the tale of a thirty-year-old woman protecting a child. Into my mind sprang an image of a woman. She was dressed for traveling and carrying a short spear. A young boy was holding her hand and running to keep up. He seemed well-bred, but strong-willed too. A million thoughts raced through my mind. He didn't look like her child. Was she taking care of him for his mother? If so, why? One idea led to another, and before I knew it, the story was finished.

Moribito: Guardian of the Spirit takes place in a land born from my imagination, and the names of the characters and places are all from languages that belong to this imaginary world. Yet it is also influenced by the culture and lifestyle of my birthplace, Japan, in some ways resembling the country in the Middle Ages.

Like a tree spreading its branches, the story of this land that lies superimposed on another world has grown and expanded so that now, thirteen years after I started, there are ten tales in all. The Moribito series, which begins with this book, has won a wide following among children and their parents in Japan. Recently, it was made into an animated series for television by the director of *Ghost in the Shell: Stand Alone Complex*. It is also a popular manga series. And now it has crossed the ocean to the United States, Italy, and Taiwan. The seed that popped into my mind thirteen years ago has grown into a very large tree indeed.

I am thrilled that *Moribito: Guardian of the Spirit* will be published and read in the United States. I hope you enjoy the adventures of Balsa, the kind-hearted, spear-wielding body-guard, and the brave, honest boy she protects in this fantasy world that carries the scent of Japan.

Nahoko Uehashi
Chiba, Japan
May 2008

This book was edited by Cheryl Klein and designed by Phil Falco. The text was set in Adobe Garamond Pro, a typeface designed by Robert Slimbach in 1989. The display type was set in Bureau Eagle, designed by David Berlow in 1990.

DISCOVER BALSA'S
NEXT ADVENTURE IN

MORIBITO II

GUARDIAN OF THE DARKNESS

Outside, the night air enveloped them, startlingly cold and smelling of snow: night's breath blowing down from the snow-capped mother range. White peaks glittered blue in the moonlight. Arrested by the familiar scent of her homeland, Balsa stopped and gazed up at the star-dusted sky.

"Er. . . ." The boy looked up at Balsa, his face faintly lit by the moon. A head shorter than her but sturdily built, he looked about fourteen or fifteen. His tunic of tanned goat hide marked him as a member of the warrior class, as did the broad knife that hung from the back of his thick leather belt. "Thank you," he said, his voice husky, as if it had only recently changed.

"Yes, well, we were just lucky to get out of there alive," Balsa replied, and then added sternly, "How could you be so stupid? Taking your younger sister into the cave to test your courage! A young man like you with the right to carry a dagger — you should have known better. She could have been killed!"

The boy looked startled. "No, you've got it all wrong!" his sister interjected. "I was the one who went in to get the stone, not my brother." Her voice was surprisingly firm and steady. Balsa had assumed she was only about ten, but she revised her estimate to twelve or even thirteen. "There's this boy in our village who's so stuck up — he keeps talking about how he's from the chieftain's line and laughing at us, and he said if *we* went into the caves to get a stone, we'd never come out alive because we're just from a branch family.

That's why I did it."

Balsa suppressed a smile. "I see. Now I understand *why* you did it. But it still wasn't worth risking your life. You should never underestimate the caves. You almost died in there tonight."

The two children said nothing, most likely reliving the terror they felt when they met the *hyohlu*. The girl shuddered on Balsa's back, and she hitched her higher up. "Don't ever go into the caves again, you understand?" She felt the girl nod. "Good. That's settled then. Is your village near here?"

"Yes," the boy responded. "I'm Kassa, son of Tonno of the Musa clan. This is my sister Gina."

His words startled Balsa. Jiguro had belonged to the Musa clan. She had never heard the name Tonno, but still, it seemed a strange coincidence that the first people she should meet after twenty-five years were from Jiguro's clan. Now she understood how he had known these caves so well. This was his territory, and that was why he had chosen this escape route all those years ago.

"Excuse me, but are you a foreigner?" Kassa asked hesitantly, interrupting her thoughts.

"What?"

"You're dressed like someone from New Yogo, and the way you talk is, well . . ."

Since Jiguro's death, she had had few opportunities to speak Kanbalese, and she now found herself searching the past for words. Apparently they had noticed it too. "No, I was born in Kanbal. But I've been on a very long journey."

As she said this, her natural instinct for caution took over. She had come back to Kanbal to find Jiguro's family and tell them the truth about why he had to escape. But before she did that, she needed to know what people thought about their flight. Royal politics and treachery had forced them to flee; to reveal her identity too soon might be very dangerous.

She looked down at the boy. "You're Kassa and Gina, right? I want you to do me a favor." Kassa nodded. "Don't tell anyone that you met me in the caves. You can tell your family that you saved Gina yourself."

It was too dark to see clearly, but she thought that Kassa looked troubled. "Can't we tell our parents?" Gina asked from her perch on Balsa's back. "If you come with us, I know they'll want to meet you and have you stay for a meal. Please come with us."

"Thank you, but I can't." Balsa had already thought of her excuse for traveling around Kanbal, and she used it now. "I'm on a journey of penance to save my foster father's soul. If I accept any hospitality from your family, my good deed won't have any effect. You know that, don't you? So please don't tell anyone that I helped you."

The children nodded, and Balsa breathed a secret sigh of relief. The people of Kanbal believed that those who died without righting their wrongs suffered eternally as slaves of the Mountain King, the mysterious ruler of the land underground. Their only hope for salvation was for one of the living to abandon home and family and wander about doing good deeds in atonement for the dead person's sins.

Balsa had no idea if this was true. She had traveled widely and found that people's beliefs about where the soul went after death differed from one country to the next. She did not really care which of these versions was right: She would find out soon enough when she died. But people doing penance might wear a red headband or even don the clothes of the opposite sex, which would explain Balsa's spear and man's attire. It was the perfect excuse. *And besides,* she thought to herself, *it's not so far from the truth.*

"Can you make it home from here on your own?" she asked. Kassa nodded. "All right, then. Oh, and by the way, what did you do with the torch?"

"I still have it, but it was snuffed out." He held it up for Balsa to see. She frowned. The usually bristly top was flat and smooth, as if it had been sliced with a sharp blade. She remembered the whistling sound and the flash of light that struck the torch. Had the *hyohlu* thrown some kind of weapon? *If so,* she thought, *it must have been very sharp and broad. And even then, could he really have snuffed out a torch in one throw?*

But this was no time to be wondering. She lowered Gina to the ground and helped her climb onto Kassa's back, then took a flint box from her bag to light the torch. She gave it to Gina and asked Kassa, "Will this last you until you reach home?"

They nodded. She could see them clearly for the first time in the light of the torch. Kassa had a boyish face and looked a little unsure of himself, but she could tell he was a serious youth who cared about his sister. Gina was dark-skinned, and her braided hair was looped on top of her head. Although there was still a trace of fear in her eyes, her firmly set lips betrayed a strong will.

"Well, I guess it's time to say good-bye," Balsa said. "I don't suppose you could tell me the quickest way from here to the nearest market?"

"That would be Sula Lassal," Kassa said. "It's about thirty *lon* from here — what you'd call an hour's walk that way, down at the bottom of the valley. It's the biggest *lassal* in Musa territory, so you'll find lots of inns."

Balsa thanked him and headed down the path, but she had no intention of staying in an inn tonight. She would camp outside and wait until several hours after sunrise, when people were up and about. Then she would go to the market to buy some local clothes. If she wanted to be inconspicuous, everything else would have to wait.

The two children watched her disappear rapidly into the darkness before they set off for home.

"Kassa . . . ," Gina whispered, "I'm really sorry."

He said nothing. *It's not something you can fix just by apologizing*, he thought.

Still, he understood why Gina had gone into the caves, and the reason had a name: Shisheem.

"Let me tell you something," Shisheem had announced that day at school. "Warriors who don't belong to the chieftain's line aren't anything more than plain soldiers. They aren't real warriors at all. That's what my father says. I'm different, you see. I can be chosen as a King's Spear, like my father, and go under the mountain to meet the *hyohlu*." He looked down at Kassa and added, "We know the secret rituals, so we're worthy of such an honor. You'd die if you tried to enter the caves."

Before Kassa could respond, Gina said hotly, "Oh, really? And you think you wouldn't? All right then — prove it! Show us a piece of *hakuma*."

Shisheem smiled gently, clearly just humoring a child. Then he put his hand into his tunic and pulled out a smooth, translucent white stone. "Here. See this? This is *hakuma*." He caressed it gently with his thumb. "Clan chieftains teach their sons the secrets when they turn fifteen. Of course I can't tell you what we do, but I've been training for over a year now. So you can dare me all you want — it's just stupid kid games to me."

His words seemed to reach Kassa from some far and lofty place. Kassa was one of the shortest boys in his clan and not particularly strong, but he made up for it by being a fast runner and a decent spear-wielder. While Shisheem was taller and stronger, Kassa could still hone his warrior skills through effort and perseverance.

But what Shisheem was talking about now was a completely different matter: There was nothing Kassa could do about his birth. The King's Spears were the highest-ranked warriors in Kanbal. They lived in the capital and acted as the king's shield and guard, his last wall of defense in event of attack. More importantly, they alone had the glorious honor of meeting the Mountain King in his underground palace, which was said to be made of luminous blue *luisha*.

But just as a commoner or a shepherd could never become a warrior, Kassa, though born to the warrior class, could never hope to become one of the nine Spears. Only direct descendants of the clan's founder could be chosen, and the right was passed from father to son. Youth from the chieftain's line went to live in the capital at the age of fifteen or sixteen, not long after they received their dagger, to devote themselves to acquiring the skills, etiquette, and knowledge required of upper-class warriors. Shisheem would likely leave for the capital soon, and one day he might even become a Spear. But Kassa would stay here in the village. Every winter he would migrate to New Yogo for work, and the rest of the year he would follow the goats with the Herder People, acting as their overlord. His skills as a warrior would only be called upon in the event of a war with another country.

Although Kassa envied Shisheem, in his heart he was resigned. But Gina was stubborn, and too young to have given up on the future. On the way home from school, she looked up at Kassa and said, "The chieftain's blood runs in our veins too, right?"

"Yes, Mother is the chieftain's younger sister," Kassa said automatically. "But warrior blood is passed from father to son. That means nothing."

"Kassa, you give up too easily!" Gina protested. "Even commoners bring back stones from the caves."

It's not bringing back a stone that's important, Kassa thought, but he didn't feel like explaining it to his sister. She fell silent, but he could guess what she was thinking.

"Don't do anything stupid, Gina."

She glared at him. "What do you mean by stupid?"

"I mean, don't even *think* about going into those caves to bring back a stone."

Before she could answer, some friends ran up and interrupted them. The rest of the day went by as usual, and Kassa forgot all about their conversation until he came home in the dark after spear practice.

Commoners in Kanbal lived in one-room houses of thick stone, with steep roofs to keep the snow off. As Kassa's family belonged to the warrior class, they had an attic, where he and Gina slept. It was the time of year when the nights grew longer and they ate just two meals a day, a late breakfast and an early dinner, to save their lamp oil. Gina had gone to bed right after supper — or at least she should have. But when Kassa saw a thick rope hanging down the outside wall from the smoke hole in the attic, he knew immediately what his sister had done.

He entered the house and, without telling his parents, went up to his room, pretending that he too was going to bed. Then he climbed down the rope and went after Gina. Before he left, he grabbed a torch from the toolshed. Then he ran all the way to the caves. As he was a fast runner, he fully expected to catch up with Gina, but he was not so lucky. By the light of his torch he could see her small footprints leading inside. He had to admire her courage; the caves were terrifying enough in the daytime. Even though she had chosen to go at night just to keep from getting caught, she was still the only girl he knew who would dare to set foot inside them after dark.

He stood anxiously at the mouth of the cave, hoping to meet her on her way out. But no matter how long he waited, she did not appear, and he grew increasingly concerned. He was sure she would have gone slowly, feeling her way along the wall so that she would not get lost. But if so, then what could be taking her so long? Various possibilities passed through his head. Perhaps she needed time to dig out a stone, or maybe *hakuma* could only be found a long way inside. But there was another possibility that stuck in his mind and stayed there: the *hyohlu*.

Unable to stand the suspense any longer, he finally went inside. With the torch in his right hand, he ran his left hand along the wall and followed Gina's footprints in the rough sand.

He was afraid to call her name in case the *hyohlu* heard. The cave gradually broadened, and soon the light of the torch began reflecting off the glittering walls. *Hakuma!* For a second, he forgot about Gina and bent to pick up a stone lying at his feet. He stood there caressing it, marveling at its smoothness. Then he tucked it into his tunic. *Really, Shisheem!* he thought. *What was the big deal about that?* He smiled to himself.

Just then, he heard Gina scream. She sounded very close. He broke into a run, following her voice. He turned a corner and his blood froze. In the light of the torch, he saw Gina lying on the ground and a black shape towering over her.

Gina! He'll eat her! But he could not reach for his dagger. Fear had rooted him to the spot. He could not even scream.

Feeling the warmth of his sister on his back, Kassa silently thanked the woman they had met. But for her, he and Gina would be dead. He realized suddenly just how precious life was. Yet the fact that he had been unable to lift even a finger to save his sister stabbed him to the heart. *I guess it's true. I don't have what it takes to be a Spear.*

As if she had heard his thoughts, Gina suddenly blurted out, "You know, that proves it, Kassa. Shisheem's a liar."

"What?"

"That lady, she fought the *hyohlu* and saved us, didn't she? She's a woman, right? So that proves you don't have to be from the chieftain's line and you don't even have to be a man to beat the *hyohlu*."

Kassa stopped in his tracks. Gina was right. "Yes," he said, "but it could have been because she wasn't afraid of dying. She's doing penance, after all."

Gina laughed. "So what? It still shows that who your parents are or whether you're a girl or a boy have nothing to do with it. I can't wait to see Shisheem's face tomorrow!"

"Wait a minute! You can't tell Shisheem that you met her. We promised to keep it a secret." He started walking again.

"Oh, right," she said, disappointed. But then she began wriggling on his back.

"Cut that out! You're heavy enough as it is without squirming around."

Gina shoved her fist under his nose. "But look! I can still get back at Shisheem! A piece of *hakuma* fell inside my tunic when the *hyohlu* got near me."

"Is that all?" Kassa started to say, planning to tell her about the piece he'd picked up himself. But a blue light was seeping out from between Gina's fingers, and he gasped instead.

She opened her hand to reveal the stone and gave a small squeak. It was not *hakuma* but *luisha*, the most precious gem in Kanbal.